ARCADE
OR HOW TO WRITE A NOVEL

D1548203

ARCADE
OR HOW TO
WRITE A NOVEL

Gordon Lish

FIC LISH
Lish, Gordon.
Arcade, or, How to write a
 novel

A NOVEL

FOUR WALLS EIGHT WINDOWS
NEW YORK / LONDON

© 1998 BY GORDON LISH

PUBLISHED IN THE UNITED STATES BY
FOUR WALLS EIGHT WINDOWS
39 WEST 14TH STREET
NEW YORK, N.Y. 10011
HTTP://WWW.FOURWALLSEIGHTWINDOWS.COM

U.K. OFFICES:
FOUR WALLS EIGHT WINDOWS/TURNAROUND
UNIT 3 OLYMPIA TRADING ESTATE
COBURG ROAD, WOOD GREEN
LONDON N22 67Z

FIRST PRINTING NOVEMBER 1998.

LIBRARY OF CONGRESS CATALOGUING-IN-PUBLICATION DATA:
LISH, GORDON
ARCADE, OR HOW TO WRITE A NOVEL : A NOVEL/GORDON LISH
P. CM.
ISBN 1-56858-115-7
I. TITLE.
PS3562.174A63   1998
813'.54—DC21   98-26693
CIP

PRINTED IN THE UNITED STATES
TEXT DESIGN BY INK, INC.
PRODUCTION BY MORGAN BRILLIANT
10 9 8 7 6 5 4 3 2 1

FOR RAFFEL

FOR KIMBALL

TO DELILLO AND DELILLO

AND GUGLIELMINA, GUGLIELMINA

AND FOR ROSIE, O ROSIE,

NON-CONSENSUAL COLLABORATOR,

BUT COLLABORATOR PAR EXCELLENCE,

IN THE PRESENT RAVAGE AND PILLAGE

A childhood
is not a period of life
and does not pass on.
It haunts discourse.

—JEAN-FRANÇOIS LYOTARD

In the game of becoming,
the being of becoming
also plays the game
with itself.

—GILLES DELEUZE

FORTY-THIRD TRY

A LATER TRY OR A TRY LATER

LAST TRY EVER TRY

A WORD FROM,
YOU KNOW,
FROM THE AUTHOR OF THIS

HOW TO WRITE A NOVEL

ARCADE
OR HOW TO WRITE A NOVEL

FORTY-THIRD TRY

THEY MADE ME THINK Aunt Lily owned it. They kept making me think it was Aunt Lily who owned it. All the way from Woodmere to Lakewood they kept saying things to me that like sounded like to me like Aunt Lily owned it. But Aunt Lily did not own it. Aunt Lily was not the owner of it. Aunt Lily just worked in the kitchen of it just making dough for the strudel for the families who got themselves into their various different automobiles and came to it. But I would not eat the strudel. I never ate the strudel. They used to bring it out steaming out from the kitchen, the strudel. You could see it, you could see it, the strudel the ladies carried out on trays still steaming out from the kitchen. The ladies used to all come out of it with the strudel on their trays still steaming out from the kitchen. One lady had a tray of it for one family's table and another lady had a tray of it for another family's table. Everybody was a family and there was a certain number of families and there was a certain number of ladies and there was a certain number of tables plus a certain number of cabins the families stayed in. But it was always only Aunt Lily who ever carried any tray of anything to my family's table. Except nobody could ever get me to eat any of the strudel. I was always all finished eating anything by the time of the strudel. All of the boy cousins always said they were always all of them too stuffed for

them to get down any of the strudel. I do not remember me ever seeing Cousin Buddy eat any or me
ever seeing Cousin Abby eat any—or Cousin Jerry or
Cousin Kenny. Did Cousin Big Eugene or did Cousin
Little Eugene, did either of them ever eat any of the
strudel? Because I do not think any of the boy cousins ever actually had anything good to stand there and
say for any of the strudel. But maybe the girl cousins
did. Except I can't for a fact say if any of the girl cousins ever actually did, but maybe they actually did and
maybe I, you know, maybe I didn't hear anybody ever
say anything about it. Myself Gordon, I was only paying attention to anything when it was the time for the
arcade. I was always thinking about this thing with
various different prizes in it which they had them at
the arcade. I only remember waiting to get pennies
from the people when it was the time for the arcade.
I only remember not being able to stand it one more
minute until I could go get up from where I was sitting and go walk around the table and go get pennies
from my father or from somebody for when it was the
time for the arcade. Did the girl cousins ever come
with us when it was the time for the arcade? I don't
remember if any of the girl cousins ever came with all
of the boy cousins when it was time for us all to get
up and go to the arcade. But they had prizes for them
as far as the girl cousins. In the thing I was telling you

about—in the Treasure Chest or in the Buried Treasure—they had prizes for people like the girl cousins down in the sand. They had a little comb for them, for instance. They had a little tiny toy mirror for them, for instance. They had a ring for them and a necklace for them and like a bracelet and probably a barrette and a ribbon in I think it was cellophane and there was a little tiny toy scissors and a thimble and some needles and I think a spool of maybe different-colored thread. But what about the medal? Wasn't there like, you know, like way over in a corner at the feet of the pirate like a, you know, like a kind of a gold-colored medal? Or was it just for boys, the medal, the medal? It could have been just for boys. It could have been a soldier thing or like that kind of thing. It could have been a sailor thing or a thing like that kind of thing. But I thought it was only for Christians no matter who it was for and that I Gordon better not ask. There were a lot of things I thought to myself in my mind I better not ask. Like I never asked what mere in Woodmere meant. I never asked didn't everyone not actually notice there was wood in Woodmere and there was wood in Lakewood and how come was that or how come was it the flowers in front of it were so lonely-looking standing there as flowers to me? Weren't they just plain yellowish flowers which shouldn't have looked so lonely-looking? And besides

which, why would flowers look so lonely-looking to
anyone whatever color the flowers were standing there
colored? They had these two rows of flowers in front.
They had this walkway with like these two rows of
flowers going around it in front. You got to the place
and everybody got out, the whole family of all of the
Lishes got out, and there was this walkway with rows
of flowers running all around it along it in front. You
walked along it and went up it and it took you to the
steps and then you went up the steps and then you
were there up on the porch. The walkway which they
had out front, it was so beautiful-looking. I think it
was really beautiful-looking—but not because of the
big white blocks which made up the border of it but
because of the flowers looking so pale-looking and
looking so lonely-looking down in the ground in between them, like these big white whitewashed blocks.
Do you see what I mean? There was a walkway with
borders along it—like a path, call it a path. There was
a sign on a pole with a lantern on it which said Laurel in the Pines. Then there was, I told you, the path.
So you started walking and walking along up the path.
I remember walking and walking along up the path.
Somebody said to me sweetheart, just keep going until you get to, you know, to the steps. Somebody said
to me sweetheart, careful careful not for you to step on
any of Aunt Lily's grass on your way along the way to

Aunt Lily's steps. But it wasn't Aunt Lily's grass and they weren't Aunt Lily's steps. The grass in front, the steps in front, none of it was Aunt Lily's. Aunt Lily didn't own any of the things in front or own any of Laurel in the Pines or even have the name Lish even. Or even Deutsch even. Aunt Lily just worked in the kitchen. It was just Aunt Lily's job to do what they told her to do in the kitchen. Aunt Lily wasn't any big deal. She was almost as small as I was. She wasn't even the boss of even the kitchen. She just cooked things and baked things and carried trays of it out to your table and picked up what the family was finished with and took it back to the kitchen. There was Uncle Charley. There was Aunt Esther. There was Uncle Sam. There was Aunt Dora. There was Uncle Henry. There was Aunt Miriam. There was my mother and my father—there namely was Philip and namely Regina. I loved them. I love them. I can't love anybody as much as I love the Lishes. They all sat around the table for the family eating. They ate everything. They ate second helpings. There wouldn't be any pennies left, there wouldn't be anybody with anymore pennies left, but there they would all of them all still be all still sitting eating in the eating hall eating second helpings of strudel, the grownups, the grownups. They never asked me how the arcade went. Nobody ever asked me how the arcade went. I was always

waiting for them to ask me for me to show us what
you got, sweetheart, show us what you got—but if any
of the grownups ever asked me about anything, I never
heard them do it, did I? I never got anything anyway.
There wasn't one prize I ever got out of the tank anyway. Not once was there ever once a prize I got all
of the way up out of the sand and then out of the tank
anyway. It was like a tank. I can't think of any word
for me to say it was like except say tank. The one
word in the English language, if you want to know
what it is, it's tank, it's tank, this is the one word. The
Treasure Chest or the Buried Treasure, it was first of
all like a tank of glass. Then on the bottom it stood
on a stand. So this is what it was like—it was like a
glass tank standing on a stand. Then you had a slot
for the penny to go in. There was this slot in it where
you stood there in front of it and put your penny in.
Then on the top there must have been a cover for it
up on the top. Something must have gone over it up
on the top—because if nothing did, if there wasn't anything which did, then couldn't people just come and
stand there and put their hands in? It was probably
iron or steel. The cover they must have had on the
top, this and the stand it stood on, they were probably
made out of, you know, out of iron or steel. Everything felt so hard in those days. Everything felt like it
was iron or steel in those days. Unless it was some-

thing which was soft-feeling—but I cannot think of anything that was soft-feeling except the flowers if you felt them and the grass. I take it back, I take it back— I felt soft. It felt soft sitting in my mother's lap and it felt soft sitting in my father's lap—but I felt softer-feeling than anything. I felt so weak. I was the youngest one of all the cousins and I was the smallest one of all the cousins and I was the weakest of them and the most scared. When the men on horses came, I was the most scared. When the men on horses with holsters with rags tied around them came, my father was scared and my mother was scared and my sister was scared, but I was the most scared. My father—I don't know, I don't know, but I think he was the second-most-scared. He's dead, my father is dead, but I think if you could ask him, I think he would be only too willing to tell you he was probably the second-most-scared. They're all dead. The whole family is dead. I am the only Lish who isn't dead. I am probably the only Lish who isn't dead—but I have to tell you, it's time I told you, I'm old. There is something else for me to tell you I left out. There is something worse than the men on horses with guns coming. But I have decided for a while to keep leaving it out. It concerns the kitchen. It concerns something which I saw through the dough when I looked up at the dough in the kitchen. You know what it concerns? It concerns when my father

took me by the hand and took me to the kitchen. It
was when we first got there. It was when the family
first got there to Laurel in the Pines for the family's
vacation. It was the first thing my father did after I was
finished with the walkway and was finished with the
steps and was up there on the porch and nobody had
done anything else at Laurel in the Pines yet. I don't
think my father had even gone to the office before
then to tell them the family was there yet. He didn't
even first check in with the office to find out from
them which cabin we were going to have yet—the one
the Laurel in the Pines people wanted our part of the
family in, my mother and my father and my sister who
was Natalie and me. Her name used to be Lorraine.
Somebody changed Natalie's name to Natalie from
Lorraine. But it was the same thing with the other girl
cousins—Ruth was Reggie and Iris was Wanda. Wait
a minute. Do you want for me to explain about Big
Eugene and Little Eugene? Because it's just that there
were two Eugenes. Uncle Charley and Aunt Esther
had a Eugene and Uncle Henry and Aunt Miriam had
a Eugene. So people called them like, you know, like
Big Eugene and Little Eugene so everybody would
know which one was which Eugene. You know what
else there was? Because there was a thing like this
with my cousin Ruth. Her name got changed from
Ruth to Reggie. You remember I said my mother's

name was Regina? My mother's name was Regina. But everybody except my father called my mother Reggie. So this made it two Reggies, didn't it? But the family didn't say Big Reggie and say Little Reggie even though there was a big age difference as far as these two different Reggies. Did anybody ever explain this? I don't know why nobody ever explained this. It would not be my way of doing things with people, not explaining things to people. I hate it when people don't go ahead and explain things to you. I hate it when people know things and don't just go ahead and explain them to you. How much trouble is it? It's not a lot of trouble. Everything would be so different for you if people would just explain things to you. The whole world would be a better place for us to live in if people just went ahead and took the time to sit you down and explain things to you. But they don't want to bother, do they? When can you ever find more than one or two of them who will ever take the time to bother? You're lucky if you can find just one or two of them, aren't you? I keep hoping I can find just, you know, just one or two of some people like that. It's what gives me the strength to keep going. It's what keeps me going as far as strength. I keep looking back to the old days and it makes me shake my head. Why did my father call my mother Reg? One of the things I would like to know is why my father called

my mother Reg. Nobody else called my mother Reg.
I never heard anybody else ever call my mother Reg.
It didn't sound nice to my ears to me. It always
sounded like there was something wrong to me in it
to my way of hearing things. But probably the same
thing goes for her calling him Phil. People in the family, they called my father Phillie, but my mother, she
called my father Phil. So I suppose it came out even-
steven between them. I just probably had not thought
it all of it out before, the fact that it really probably
worked out pretty even-stevenly between them. It's
just that Reg sounds to me worse-sounding to me than
Phil does. Doesn't somebody saying Reg sound
worse-sounding to you than them saying Phil does?
But I suppose it all comes about upon your specific
way of thinking. Probably no two people have the
same specific way of thinking. When I tell you about
what was for instance up in the ceiling, when I tell
you about what I for instance could see through the
dough when I looked through it and could see, you
know, could see up to the ceiling, maybe nobody but
me will be able for them to see any reason for anybody to stand there and be scared of it. You might
think he is silly. You might think he is making a mountain out of a molehill. You might think he should go
get his head examined or go check himself into like an
insane asylum, an individual to be so scared of some-

thing which is probably in millions and millions of the most normal kitchens. But I know what I saw and do you? No, you don't! Okay, okay, but I would like to know who is to say we will ever come to terms about it. Human beings just don't see things the same specific way. Anything, you name anything, no two human beings are ever going to stand there and see it the same specific way. This is why the world is in the shape it's in. This is why it could drive you crazy, the shape which everything which happens in the world is in. But we have to accept it. It is our lot, as they say, for us as human beings to sit here and accept it. We can't sit around bewailing it and bemoaning it. It does no good for us to sit around and spend all of our time just, you know, just bewailing it and bemoaning it. It wears me out the way people behave. I find it very fatiguing. I hate to say it, I really hate to say it but, I'm sorry, it's very fatiguing for me. I wish we could all of us as human beings just look on the bright side of things. Everybody would be so much happier if they could just say to themselves I'm going to do my best to sit down and look on the bright side of things. Take the trip to Lakewood. Even just the name of it itself should make normal people feel good, shouldn't it? Just listen to it, Lakewood. Did you ever hear a prettier name for a place than Lakewood? Or how about Laurel in the Pines? That's beautiful. Listen to

how beautiful-sounding it is, Laurel in the Pines. So
you tell me—so why does it upset me so much? I
would really like for someone to make it their business to come and tell me why it upsets me so much.
Because if it's because I thought it was Aunt Lily's and
it turned out not for it to be Aunt Lily's, then is this
fair to either the name of the place or to either myself? It's not justified. This is my point, that it is
strictly not justified. Yet here I am, an aged person,
whose most positively wonderful experience in their
whole life was his trip to Lakewood, was this trip to
Laurel in the Pines in Lakewood, and yet how can I as
an honest person sit here and not be honest with you
about the fact that even the names themselves, they
make me feel uneasy-feeling? I'm trying to explain it.
Do you hear me trying to explain it? Respect me as
a human being at least for the fact that what am I sitting here doing is trying to explain it. But can I explain it? I can't even explain it to myself, let alone sit
here and explain it to you. So okay, so is it all just the
wood and the trees—and, you know, and the idea of
a lake? Is this what you think it is, that it's this? Because I don't think so. My God, I loved the out-of-
doors. I was all for it for the out-of-doors. When I
saw the flowers in front, when I saw the rows of the
flowers in front, I said to myself look how beautiful-
looking this is, these flowers in front. I had a feeling.

I'm telling you I had this feeling. I was swept away. We got out of the car and the family was getting all of the luggage out and somebody said to me sweetheart, just keep going to the steps. It was thrilling for me. I never saw such grass as that. I never saw such grass like that. I never felt so good. You, what about you, you would have felt the same way too. There was this walkway you walked along. They had it marked out for you so you couldn't miss it as far as walking along it. It was all arranged for you in advance. They had thought it all out for you in advance. I think the word for this is border or borderline. They had these white-washed blocks of something. They had these blocks which were whitewashed and were made out of some-thing and then there would be like a space between them and then a flower. They were on both sides of you. You had them going along with you on both sides of you—like a whitewashed block and then a space and then, you know, and then a yellowish flower—so pale-looking and so lonely-looking and so fragile-looking. You just wanted to just lie down and just cry. No, I don't like that. Cry's not the right idea in my mind for that. This is what is so terrible, so ter-rible with things when you sit down and say to your-self I am going to sit here and go ahead and, you know, and write it up, a thing like this. I mean, your mind is going along and your mind is going along and

you just don't stop to give any one particular specific
thing enough thought in it. For instance, I should be
thinking what did I really feel like doing, was it cry-
ing or was it just lying down or was it something else?
You can't believe it how good my memory is of the
feeling itself but not of what I felt like doing. Because this is the thing, isn't it? It's not what what a
human being feels—it is what a human being feels like
doing. It's just like I just got out of the rumble seat
and I hear them say just keep going until you get to
the steps, sweetheart, and there's the grass and there's
the path and there's the rows of flowers and these
blocks of whitewashed blocks. But where was Natalie?
Or, you know, or Lorraine? Because wasn't it both of
us, weren't we both of us in the rumble seat? Or
hadn't we been? I want to say daffodils. There is this
feeling I have which makes me feel I have to say it was
daffodils. But I do not know the first thing about
flowers. All I know is some of the words for flowers.
So when I say daffodils, don't think this means daffodils were the flowers they were. No, I would not go
as far as to say they were daffodils as flowers. But the
word daffodils, it is the word daffodils which sounds
like to me like what they looked like to me. Or I
suppose what I better say is how now they do, how
now they do—when I look back at it in my mind with
my mind's eye. That or dahlias maybe or jonquils.

These words sound like what the feeling of them was like to me when I first got out of the rumble seat and starting walking along between them, which is to say like these two winding rows of them—dahlias or jonquils. Maybe sort of like daffodil-feeling flowers. Wait a minute, wait a minute. I think I am going too fast again. Because they were more like gently curving actually and not so winding actually. A pair of rows, you might say, this pair of gently curving rows, you might say, which kept you on—this is a joke I'm making, this is just a little joke to myself which I am making—which kept you on the straight and narrow. With the help of, you know, of the whitewashed blocks, of course. It really marked the whole thing out for you— the walkway you went along to get to the steps and not step on the grass. So that you had to really be a person that would not be paying attention for you to wander off and get lost. Does delphinium fit the bill, do you think? Or would this be a different kettle of fish as far as your feeling for this, delphinium? It first just occurred to me to try out delphinium. But this would be the ear in my mind which is listening to this and not the eye in it seeing. Look, everything I can do for me to keep things going along—here we go again, only not this time so much as a joke this time—on the straight and narrow I am doing. I hope you notice. Because it builds up to our advantage if you notice.

There is a definite mutual advantage for us if we keep working together with each other with clarity and candor. So when I say delphinium sounds to me like it might have been the flowers the Laurel in the Pines people had planted in the ground for you so there would be like a borderline made up of blocks and of flowers for you and you, you know, you wouldn't make a mistake and go outside of it, I am just reacting to the feelings I have about things and not to any like specific particular knowledge upon it. It's the same reason I said steel or iron. It's the same reason arcade is like the whole beginning of everything for me—the word arcade or arcade as a word. Abby was the one I first heard first say it. That's what I think, Abby. Remember my cousin, Cousin Abby? His name was actually Abbott. We called him Abby or Abs. Maybe not everybody in the family called him Abby or Abs, but a lot of them did—call him either Abby or Abs and never Abbott. He was the cousin next to me in age. If you go up from the youngest to the oldest—who was Cousin Big Eugene, by the way, who was Cousin Big Eugene—if you count upwards, Abby, or Abs, was the next cousin next up from me. He was sweet. He was so sweet. You know what I remember Abby always saying to me when we would all be running, all of the cousins, or all anyhow all of us boy cousins, when we would all of us boy cousins would all be running from the eating hall to hurry and get to the arcade? Don't fall over anything, Gordie, don't fall! And something else, and something else—Abby was the only one who would. It shows such a sweet nature. Don't you think it shows such a sweet nature? I think it shows the sweetest of human natures. I was the smallest and I thought look at me, look at me— aren't I lucky to have a cousin who has such a sweet nature? Well, I mean I think that's what I must have thought. Because it would be like me for me to think a thing like this. But probably I did not think with words of this kind of character back then in those old days. You know what I'm saying? My words were not the words of now. So how old was I then? I can hear you weighing the question of how old was I personally then. It would be perfectly natural for you as a reader to at this point ponder about this. I'm thinking. I'm pondering over it too! I'm sitting here giving it due consideration. Believe me, I do not want to make the same mistake I made when I said cry. You see what happens? I went too fast and didn't say the right thing and now I can't think of the right thing even though I know the first thing's wrong. This is what happens, this is what happens—now the wrong thing's got the right one down under underneath it. This is why I am taking my time. I'm going to go along and go along very methodically now. I was go-

ing too fast. Now I am not going to go along so fast.
The only problem with going along like I am going
to go now is this problem of running out of time. But
look at life, look at life—it's always the problem of
running out of time. I had a girlfriend once and this
was the problem with her—the factor of running out
of time with her. We hardly had any time at all. Hey,
is it all right for me to say it was at Abby's place?
Okay, it was at Abby's place. But it wasn't where he
lived. It was this place which Abs had for when he
had girlfriends come around of his own. You know
what I mean? You know what I mean. Come on, I
probably don't have to spell it out for you, do I?
These people are all passed away now, but you have to
show respect for the dead. I don't know. Maybe Abs
didn't have the place for such a long time for it to rep-
resent a family disgrace. You could probably say it was
just a passing phase for him, having this place. We all
have these passing phases. For instance, didn't I out-
grow the thoughts I used to have when my father
would stand there and say Reg but everybody else
said Reggie? I think it was just a passing phase of me
being a human being. Can I tell you something?
There was somebody in the family who used to say to
somebody else in the family consider yourself kissed
whenever people in the family were all getting together
and, you know, and kissing hello. I'm telling you, this

used to make me so distressed. I experienced a great deal of distress in myself from it. But do I do so anymore? Ask me if I do so anymore. Because I know you know I do not do so anymore. These things get outgrown, don't they? They are just passing phases in the passing parade. There was once something somebody once said once which was even worse than consider yourself kissed, but you know what? It's just as outgrown. It just would run off my back like a duck now if I heard somebody say it. It wouldn't get under my skin. It would just be like a duck running off of my back to me now if I heard anybody say it about anybody else. I wouldn't sit here and get hurt feelings for the person the way I used to get them. Praise be to the heavens I am no longer the sensitive individual which once I was. Sensitive? Listen, I have to tell you something—sensitive was my middle name! If I heard the least thing, if somebody said the least thing, it would put me in such a state. It's terrible when somebody is sensitive out of all proportion to everything else. It is such a hardship. People ought to spend more time thinking about the other person. Their feelings should be uppermost in people's minds. It's the other person's feelings which we as individuals should go ahead and take into account before we just start lashing out without, you know, without proper thought. Look, try to remember they are human beings too! Always try to give them the benefit of the doubt. The people who invented the Treasure Chest, for example, or the Buried Treasure, you could get really irked with them if you did not stop to think. But ask yourself is it worth it? It's not worth it. First of all, it's not going to change anything, is it? Second of all, what about, you know, what about their point of view? I mean, suppose like everybody who came and stood there and put a penny in walked away with a prize. They'd be out of business, wouldn't they? Suppose everybody who came and put in a penny in got a compass or a pocket watch. Even if all they got was like just the top, for instance, or the little tiny toy speedboat, it still wouldn't make any sense from a dollars and cents business point of view if everybody came along and got something out of the tank, would it? There have to be restrictions. It has to be hard for people. You have to have a time limit. You can't just have the grapple bucket like come on down there and grab something for everybody and then let all comers just go ahead and walk away with a prize. Look at it from the other person's way of looking at things. To be fair to people in life, you have to try to take a look at things from, you know, from the other person's way of looking at things, no matter how disgusting to your own particular specific philosophy of life. Human beings are so self-centered. All they want to do is go look at it from their own self-advantage. But you can't do that. It's not being fair to humanity for you to do that. No, you have to look at it from the perspective of the other individual involved, be they friend or foe. You have to say to yourself I know what's in it for me, but like okay so what's in it for them? This and this alone is what a healthy mind is. It looks at things from this, you know, this like balanced perspective. What's wrong with the human race is they are too quick to discount the dollars and cents business point of view. Remember this—somebody had to make the Treasure Chest machine in the first place. Unless they called it the other one—the, you know, the Buried Treasure namely. That costs money. Somebody has to go out and lay out the loot for the raw materials. Don't forget what's involved. There's glass. There's sand. There's the steel or the iron for the cover on the top of it and for the stand and for the slot and for the handle. There's probably the motor or the spring down somewhere inside of it, right? Which must be a pretty big item for somebody to pay for, a motor or a spring. And then what about, don't forget about just as big items as those probably, don't forget—namely all of the things you need for you to get the grapple bucket set up and going—like wouldn't there be cables and things?—things like, you know, like maybe beams and maybe rods? I don't know. But, anyway,

somebody's got to go ahead and lay out the loot for all
of that. Doesn't somebody have to dig down into their
jerkin for them to stand there and come up with the,
you know, with the loot for all of that? And what
about the prizes themselves? You know what some of
them were? How would you like to hear what some
of them were? Because I happen to be positive they
had in the tank—well, what did I just say already?
Didn't I just say a pocket watch and a compass at least?
And here's more for you which I just thought of—
namely a penlight, a jackknife, a magnifying glass, a
rabbit's foot, a whistle, a key chain, and like what they
called like a Chinese puzzle. Not that all of these
were, okay, were, you know, were so expensive. I
don't know. Listen, I am just mainly guessing. But
the thing I can definitely sit here and guarantee you is
there definitely was this little tiny doll of like a pirate
standing in the corner in one of the corners in the
sand. They had him all outfitted. He just stood there
with his sword out all outfitted. He had a little tiny
eyepatch and I think probably a little tiny bandana.
But anyway, okay okay okay, just add all these things
up, okay? And don't forget to take the time to give
some thought to the fact of what they also had for
girls, for girls. Things don't come for free, do they?
Things cost people up the whatsis, don't they? The
medal alone, the medal alone—what about what they

probably had to go into hock for for the medal alone?
I don't think either one of us happens to be in a personal position to say what the business people behind
the scenes had to lay out for the medal alone, let alone
for the whole deal—and then turn around and show
a decent profit on it. Or do you think the owners of
something don't have a right to show a decent profit
on it? Maybe you think the owner of Laurel in the
Pines didn't have a right to go ahead and show a decent profit on it. Or what about my father in his business and my uncles in theirs? How was the Lish family
supposed to be able to afford to go from places like
Woodmere to Lakewood and then stay there at Laurel
in the Pines and pay for the gas to get there and have
cars and things in the first place and even just have
clothes for people to wear or have pennies to hand
over to the children when the strudel started coming
out from the kitchen steaming and you were allowed
not to have to stay there at the table and could get up
from your place and could go run with the rest of
them to the arcade instead? You know what I wonder?
I wonder if we really always ran. When I think back
in my mind to going to the arcade and so on, my
mind tells me we were always running, we always
ran—that it was the only way the cousins ever got
there in my mind when we all of us went after we ate
to the arcade. But it only stands to reason that's

wrong, it's wrong. Maybe we ran some of the time or maybe we ran some of the way, but it stands to reason to me it is wrong for you to think in your mind you ran all of the way all the time to anywhere. Besides, did all of the cousins? Did every single cousin? Don't forget, you're not forgetting, are you?—there were lots of cousins—like Kenny, like Buddy, like Jerry, and myself—then Abby and the Eugenes. Neither have we actually gone ahead yet and totally eliminated Natalie and Reggie and Wanda yet, have we? I'm seeking clarity, you know. I am making a bid for clarity, you know. On the other hand, we have to come to terms with the fact that, criers weepers, losers keepers, there is always going to be a certain amount of ducks and drakes involved with a situation when you sit down and start taking to task your memory. It's best for us to concede this right off the bat. It's best for us to come to grips with what a human being is grappling with when they dare to play hounds and hares with a thing like a person's memory. The most candid thing I can at this stage state to you is what choice did I have? There was no choice. I had no choice. It's all my mind can think about the older I get. You keep trying to get your mind to think about something else, but if you do not have the television on or if you do not have the radio on or if you are not reading the newspaper or talking to various different individuals on the telephone, then here it comes again, I'm serious—here comes again the trip the Lishes took to Laurel in the Pines again, plus the fact that the first thing your mind wants to ponder about is how come all the way from Woodmere to Lakewood everything they sat in the front seat saying made it seem to me like Aunt Lily owned it and that she wasn't just a member of people working there as like the kitchen staff. Somebody should look up mere. Okay, it should probably be me who looks up mere. But I do not think we have that kind of a dictionary here. We probably have just the kind of a dictionary where the chances are it would only tell you what mere means as far as when we say mere this or mere that. But mere as far as Woodmere, mere as far as the name of Woodmere, take my word for it, this dictionary never even dreamed of being a dictionary like this. But maybe it doesn't have any meaning, mere like this. Since when do names of places have to mean things? Lots of things don't have to have a specific particular meaning, not just names, you know. This is one of the major stumbling blocks for human beings. They get this idea in their minds. They ask themselves the question okay what is the meaning of this? They never stop to think could this be like a wild goose chase or not. They refuse to believe it's conceivably geese and ganders. This is why you have to make allowances for so many things of all varieties.

The medal, for instance—I was afraid even to ask anybody what is it a medal for. Can you believe this?
But it's the truth, it's the truth. We act like such nin-
nies on a one-to-one basis. Granted, how old was I?
Let's face it, I was the merest stripling of a child. I
myself was no more than the merest sprout of a child.
Even so, even so, is this an excuse for me being afraid
for me to even ask? I was such a child when I was a
child. Because it could maybe have been from something from the, you know, from the Christian religion.
You couldn't get it anyway. There was no way for you
to get the grapple bucket to come down to get anywhere near it anyway. They had it too close to this
little tiny doll which they made look like a pirate. It
was right at the feet of the little tiny pirate, the medal,
the medal. His sword was in the way. The grapple
bucket would like get itself pushed off-course off to
the other way somewhere on account of the sword
being in your way. Or do you say buccaneer? You can
probably tell a lot of difference between people as to
which they, you know, they say. I myself, I like saying buccaneer better. I started off saying pirate. I admit the fact that I started off like saying pirate. But it's
like when I said way back at the beginning cry. Because now I want to change it, except this time you
know what? This time I know just the way I want to
change it—to buccaneer, to buccaneer. Unless priva-

teer is really better. But does privateer mean the same thing? Because it just popped into my head just like that—privateer. Just, you know, like just pop. Well, you say arcade, the next thing you know, here comes cascade, here comes serenade, here comes so forth and so on. Cavalcade. Masquerade. Cry was not right. Cry was close, but definitely not right. Lie down, however—lie down was right, however. You know what I would have to say? I would have to say lie down was right on the money. Because it's no trouble at all for me to sit here and to situate myself right there right where it was at the time—the path, the path. So when I say lie down was good as gold, I believe I can honestly say I know whereof I speak. Or even fall down, like in somebody having for them to hold onto the earth. But can you see what a sensitive person I was? My nature was so extremely sensitive. My mother and father always said to me this was why I went to lengths. They always said to me Gordon, this is why you are always going to too many lengths. To this day you could still say I go to too many of them. My foot, for example, the fact that I am sitting here with a hurt foot, for example, all it is is from me going around the block, right? But I did it when I should not have done it. I'm serious. I walked when I should not have walked. I took a stroll when I should not have taken a stroll. I went out for

a breath of air when I should not have gone out for a
breath of air. I told myself Gordon, go get some exercise and a breath of air when I should not have told
myself this. But would I listen to reason? Nothing on
earth could, you know, could stop me. This is just
what they used to say to me, my mother and father,
that there was no force on earth which could keep me
from doing it, even though it wasn't the opportune
moment for me to be doing it, whatever it was, whatever the it in that particular specific case was—take a
walk, run to the arcade, even though it was maybe not
the most opportune moment for me to attempt to do
it, take a walk, run to the arcade. But this is my personality. You know what I mean? I mean, let's face it,
as a human being, I'm sorry, but this is my personality. God love them, my mother and father, may they
rest in peace, my mother and father—because they
both of them could have sat here in my place and told
you themselves Gordon's personality is he's always going to lengths, he is always going to extremes, you cannot argue with him when he gets like this. You cannot argue with me when I get like this. You would be
wasting your time for you to stand there and try to argue with me when I get like this. Which is another
reason why I am not in such a big hurry for me to go
attempt to look up mere even though I am positive it
won't be there—namely because I have my foot up on

a cushion up on a stool. So now you know—and, hey, I suppose you realize how hard it is for somebody to sit here and write like this, I suppose. Try it yourself sometime! If you, you know, you doubt me, if you cannot give me full faith and confidence, then I happen to have a little recommendation for you, if you please—go ahead and try it yourself sometime. Or is it full credit and confidence? Maybe it is full credit and confidence. Look, in regards to certain expressions, it can get pretty confusing when a person's confidence is not just at that particular specific time up to par. Your mind tells you it's this, your mind tells you it's that. A lot of it is the family you come from. A lot of it is like the nature of the family they threw the dice and you happen to come from. Did I tell you about consider yourself kissed? Isn't it unbelievable, consider yourself kissed? Hey, who do you think they stood there and said it to and who said it, who said it, do you think? But it could have been just a joke. People get together in a family like that on a trip like that, isn't it one of the things they do, start sitting around turning everything into a joke? You know what happens? I'll tell you what happens. They put their best foot off to the side. They think to themselves it's okay, this is a vacation, I'm going to go ahead and, you know, put my best foot off to the side. Everything starts going by the board. Good manners start going by the board and falling to the wayside. One of the people starts it and then all of the other people think to themselves I probably should just go ahead and join in. Before you know it, they all are all egging each other on. They're chiming in, the expression is. The next thing you know, they go too far. Somebody—it could be anybody, it could be anybody—hears somebody say something they definitely should not hear. Of course, as I say, there was the occasion in my life when I was really pretty sensitive to things. You know what I say? I say thank heavens those days are gone for good. It rolls right off my back like a duck now as of the current time. But I can remember when if I heard somebody say consider yourself kissed and the whole family was meanwhile all kissing everybody hello, I would feel so awful for this individual I could just, you know, just want to fall down on the ground and cry. Because everybody is a human being. Listen, I can tell you a worse one. I know a worse one. You want to hear a worse one? How about this one?—quote, unquote, what's the point to him, I don't see the point to him, will somebody please come tell me what's the point to him? Granted, to the best of my ability to recollect anything, any one of any number of people in the family could have said this and it could have been said in regards to any one of any number of people in the family. All I know is it was in the eating hall where I heard it when all of the Lishes past and present all went to Laurel in the Pines in, you know, in Lakewood. Look, it didn't kill anybody, did it? The fact of the matter is that it did not kill anybody for that person to have to have it said about them, did it? We have to remind ourselves, as hurtful as these experiences are for a person at the time of their occurrence, in the long run did anybody die from it, was there anybody who got killed from it? Not that I am not fully prepared to sit here and acknowledge it is the way of human beings for them to always blow things out of proportion at the time of their occurrence but then for them to later on sit themselves back and think better of it. You know something? Can I tell you something? People can't help how they are. It takes them a lot of time for them to come to their senses. You have to go along with this. Take my foot, for instance—could anything stop me? It already hurt me after only one block, but would I heed my own personal better judgment in the matter? Nothing was going to make me heed it, was it? I'm sorry, but what was to keep me from just turning around and just, you know, just coming home? Even if I had gone as much as a block and a half already, wouldn't I still be way ahead of the game if I had just turned around like an intelligent individual with the brains they were born with and come home?

To go around the block, as the expression goes, it is
how many all in all of blocks total? Okay, so it's four
blocks total. So so long as you haven't gone two
whole blocks yet, turning around still puts you in the
plus column as far as, you know, as far as total distance
walked. People are their own worst enemy. You really have to laugh, don't you? The best advice I can
give is use the brains you were born with and take
them with a grain of salt. Myself, I tend to get like
overexcited. Call it a family trait. Because there is not
one Lish I can remember who did not always go totally overboard about things. You know what they all
lost? They all lost all proportion. I'm serious. But
my mother, you know, she was actually a Deutsch.
They were probably actually calmer. But I didn't know
any of them except for her. My mother cleaved to my
father. This is what the family said. They said she
cleaved to him. She put aside the house of her youth.
She used to always say to me I came to your father with
only the clothes on my back. My mother was always
saying to you you know what I came to your father
with? And then she would say to you with only the
clothes on my back. My father did the same thing—
like ask you a question like that and then answer it for
you. There were lots of similarities as far as their per-
sonalities as far as my opinion. But in regards to the
occasion in which the men on horses came to the door

of the cabin with the holsters they had with, you know, with guns in them and like with these wrappings which went around them like bandages wrapped around them, my mother and my father behaved themselves like two totally different individuals. It was like night and day. They were like night and day. Even afterwards, even when everybody was all talking all about it in the eating hall at the family table, you could tell they were keeping their own counsel about it in totally different ways. People at the other tables, you could hear them all saying it was proof, it was proof, wasn't it proof for you of how lucky the Jews are, soldiers all of the way out in the country a million miles from everywhere practicing with their guns and their horses and their holsters for the United States Army of America? You could hear all of the other families at all of the other tables all saying thank God, thank God, all it was was only just the soldiers of the United States Army of America and not robbers, thank God, and not bandits, thank God—please God it was only for the good of the Jews and not hoodlums or worse. But you know what Cousin Big Eugene said? Cousin Big Eugene said they weren't soldiers, they weren't soldiers, they were troops. Cousin Kenny said it was a bivouac. Cousin Buddy said it was a case of the troops being on bivouac on maneuver, or maybe on bivouac on maneuvers. My mother and my father, they did not have anything to say. They just sat and ate. Then the strudel started coming out from the kitchen steaming. Then the cousins all got up to get pennies. I kept thinking in my mind ask Abby. I mean, in regards to on bivouac on maneuver or on maneuvers. But what if one thing led to, you know, to another? What if Abby asked you a question for every question you asked Abby? What if Abby said to me if I tell you, then you tell me? What if I had to tell him what my mother said for my father to do and that he did it, he did it? But didn't I do it too? Didn't we all of us but my mother do it too? I don't know. I like disremember. Isn't there the word disremember? I'm positive there is the word disremember. Even if my dictionary does not have disremember in it, this is not conclusive, is it? I'll tell you something. You want to know something? There are dictionaries and there are dictionaries. Just because one dictionary says something, don't think that's it and that's it as far as dictionaries. You have to bear something in mind. You have to bear the fact in mind that guess what—people make them! You have to bear in mind dictionaries didn't make themselves. And I don't have to tell you what people are like, do I? Believe me, I would be the first individual to say I wish with all my heart they weren't. No kidding, it honestly grieves me for me to have to sit here and say these things. I derive like not one

shred of pleasure from it. You think I sit here relish-
ing it? There is not a night which goes by that I Gordon do not get down on my knees and pray to God
above in hopes it will all turn out, you know, all turn
out different. But you can't wave a wand. The dam-
age has been done. I had every option. You cannot
stand there and say it was not a case of free will.
There was not anyone who came along who put a gun
to my head and who said to me didn't you make up
your own personal mind you were taking a walk
around the block?—so inasmuch as this is what I as a
free white American over the age of twenty-one did,
then okay, then come what may, there is no use changing it and carrying on about it. Except come what may
came! This is the thing—that come what may came!
And now look, now look. I Gordon have to sit here
with like my foot up on a stool with like a cushion.
Not that I would go look up disremember anyway.
You think I care what the dictionary says? I don't care
what any dictionary says. There is not a dictionary in
the world I would trust as far as I could spit. They're
not so high and mighty, believe me. Everybody would
be so much better off if they went ahead and devel-
oped more perspective about this. If people would
just take the time to give the age-old perspective some
more enlightened consideration. But you know what?
It's hopeless, it's hopeless. Or do you think if I Gor-

don wasn't so old I wouldn't sit here like an idiot saying this? Because I want for you to know I am absolutely open to intelligent criticism. Listen, am I infallible? Do you think I think I am infallible? I am not
infallible. I am not perfect. If I ever gave you to think
I Gordon believe myself to be, you know, to be above
criticism, then I couldn't be more apologetic. Because
it was not my intention. Not in a million years was it
my intention. Is there a better example than my foot?
If I was so perfect, would I be sitting here suffering to
beat the band like this with my foot like this? Listen,
I place the blame on going to lengths. You know what
I place the blame on? I place it on me going to
lengths. I am too much of an extremist, plain and
simple. To tell you the brutal truth, if I can tell you the
brutal truth, the shoemaker said to me Mr. Lish, my
advice to you is please don't do it. But I come from
the school where you say to yourself if one spoonful
of the medicine is good for you, then why not go
ahead and be smart and take the whole bottle? This
is my nature. This is why my mother and father were
always throwing up their hands saying the child has no
sense of proportion in him and this, God help us, is
his nature. The upshot is I'm sorry but I am an extremist. They warned me. Believe me, they did their
best to warn me and to spare no effort to curb the ten-
dency. But they were talking to a brick wall. I'm

sorry, your nature is your nature. Going to lengths, it was always my nature. You take the fact of the handle, for instance—okay, it hurt my hands, I had to use both hands, it was too big for my hands, but would I listen, would I listen, would I listen to, you know, to reason? This is probably why I sit here feeling in my mind it was iron, it felt like iron, it all was iron-feeling. Or steel. Nevertheless, I still feel it could have been rigged. I am not entirely convinced they did not have it rigged. Every meal after every supper all of us cousins except the girl cousins always got up and got pennies and went there, every single solitary meal, but when did I ever with my own two personal eyes ever see one cousin ever get the pocket watch or get the compass? Okay, okay, I do not know what anyone for a fact ever got, not any of the cousins, because okay, I admit it, I admit it, maybe some of them must have got something. But I Gordon am prepared to go with you to any court of law and swear on a stack of bibles no cousin of mine ever once walked away with the compass, for instance, or the pocket watch—and the same goes, I can bet you, I can bet you, for the jack-knife and for the penlight and for the magnifying glass—not to mention probably even the whistle. The necklace, fine, fine, that's what somebody got and, you know, and, my God, the barrette. Granted, we have to see it from the standpoint of the people who maybe

invested their life savings in it. Just the mechanical
machine itself, just the Treasure Chest or the Buried
Treasure as an investment itself, not to mention what
it must have set back the owners for the prizes, and
then, you know, then somebody comes along, then
one of the Lish cousins comes along and goes ahead
and gets the necklace, for instance—for a penny, they
get a whole necklace or barrette, for instance, for, okay,
for only a penny? And what about the owner of the
arcade itself? Isn't there somebody who has to own
the arcade itself? So does it or does it not stand to reason the owner of the arcade, this individual sees fit for
him to charge the owner of the Treasure Chest or let's
say of the Buried Treasure like a certain amount of
money on a probably a week-to-week or maybe a
month-to-month basis? Unless it was maybe like a
private family arrangement. Like with Abby with me—
like a, you know, like a private family arrangement on
a personal basis between us. Actually, Abs didn't even
make me pay him for the copies of the keys. Which
just goes to show you my point about it being on a
personal basis between us as members of the same family. Abs had to have copies made, right? The man had
to go out and actually have copies of the keys made,
right? But I'm telling you something—it is definitely
to his credit as a family member, not to mention as a
human being, that Abs did not venture to try and pass

along the cost of the copies to me. Hey, you want an example of how we Lishes were? Because this is an example of how we Lishes were. You really have to give us credit. Honestly, we had this really great family of a lot of people, and then you know what? Poof, before you know it, everybody's dead. I'm serious, the whole kit and caboodle, they're all dead. Did I tell you we all lived in Woodmere? Look, there are a lot of names of towns, there are all kinds of names of towns, there are millions and millions of names of towns, but all kidding aside, don't you think Woodmere is a pretty terrific one? I love it, I really love it—Woodmere. Which is why I honestly cannot get over the fact that the one trip of my youth when the whole Lish family as a family goes on a trip somewhere, it's to where? I mean, is it to Lakehurst, which turns out to be, you know, to be the next town over, or is it to Lakewood? So is this something or is this something? Because I happen to think you have to go ahead and give full faith and credit to a fact like this. Because I happen to think it is a mistake for you to sit there and give me the impression you are taking a fact like this for granted. God in heaven above goes to a lot of trouble getting things to, you know, to work out like this. What's wrong with people is they stand there and do not, they definitely do not appreciate. Myself, let me tell you something—because I never personally appreciated it until this minute the favor Abs did for me when he went ahead and let me use his place when I had this, you know, call it this girlfriend which I once had. And did the man ask for me to reimburse him for what he had laid out for me for him to get a set of keys made into copies for me? Answer me this, did Abs, as a cousin, ask me Gordon for one red cent in regards to the expenses which he incurred on himself? This is the meaning of family! Did you hear me? This is what we talk about when we talk about the meaning of family! You ask me why I sit here and get myself so upset with the status of things in the world of today and I have to answer you—it's because where is the meaning of family anymore? So did you hear me or did you hear me? Because if you require another example, I will be only too happy and glad to give you another example. Such as the fact that one of the keys gets bent in the lock, okay? So okay, so there's one of the keys which gets bent in one of the locks. So you're rushing around like some kind of a, you know, like some kind of a psycho, you're always racing around in a rush like, you know, like some kind of a psycho, so then what? So then there's this key that gets itself bent, that's what! But fine, fine—isn't this just the kind of a thing which is going to happen when you've got yourself a total of five keys and five locks, when you have got for yourself a total of as many

as a total of as many as five keys and five locks for you
to work them in? Hey, it's bound to, it's bound to.
It's just the mathematics of it, isn't it or isn't it? But
does Cousin Abs come to me with the charges? Does
Cousin Abs say to me Gordon, here are the charges,
take care of the charges? Do I ever hear one peep
from the man as far as what I Gordon legitimately owe
him for A, for fixing the lock, and B, for B, for getting
another copy of the key in question made? Not one
peep, mind you, not one! And what would I have
done, ask yourself what would I Gordon have done if
Cousin Abby had not made to me like a gift of his
premises? That's cousins for you. This is family for
you. And it is, for your information, what I personally
miss so much I do not even know what I am doing
half of the time, this is how sick I am from the, you
know, from the situation of the disappearance, if you
will, of, you know, of the Lish family. Yet don't think
I am complaining about me being the last Lish. Yes,
yes, yes, yes, it is a very lonely-feeling situation for me,
to be sure. All the same, I am not so unintelligent an
individual as for me to sit here and not be well aware
of the fact of what the alternative is. Or would it be
better for me to say would be? Look, you know what
words I once got out of the dictionary when I was
looking up all of the words which, you know, which
ended in ade? How about harlequinade and gascon-

ade? How do you like that?—harlequinade and gasconade! I wrote them all of them down. I said to
myself Gordon, you owe it to yourself and you owe it
to Abs, write them all of them down. Every ade word
I ever found, I sat there and wrote them all of them
down somewhere and was saving it, the list. Because
it's really something, isn't it? Like starting from some
little acorn like that like arcade and then one day, behold, behold, a mighty, you know, elm! I have to give
thanks. There is not a night when I do not give thanks
to God in heaven above. No, I never got what I
wanted whenever I put my penny in. The time was
always running out on me whenever I put my penny
in. I could never get my hands to get the handle to
get the grapple bucket to get me anything whenever I
put my penny in. But do I hold it against God in
heaven above like some individuals I could name
would? Do you think I am sitting here saying to myself this is God's fault as far as my foot having to be
up on a cushion up on a stool? Let me tell you something. Can I tell you something? I give thanks for the
cushion! I give thanks for the stool! Hey, if you want
to know the truth, the truth is I give thanks for sitting
anywhere saying anything, let alone in a nice clean
situation apropos of what I personally happen, with
God's backing, to have. Say what you want about my
situation, one thing you would have to say for it is it's

spic and span, it's clean as a whistle, you could eat off
the floor of it from stem to stern. You could get right
down on your hands and knees and go ahead and eat
right off of it. I'm proud of this. I don't mind telling you, I'm proud as, you know, as punch of this.
There are a lot of individuals who would discount it.
There are a lot of individuals who would look at it and
discount it. Beside which, how do I know if you personally are not one of them? Do I have any way of
sitting here and knowing? Fine, fine, you say you're
not, you sit there and say to me Gordon, trust me, trust
me, I swear to you I'm not. But what is the proof?
Where is the proof? Believe me, I am trying to trust
you, I am doing my level best to trust you, I am strain-
ing every shred of decency in me—but, I'm sorry, I'm
sorry, show me the proof! Okay, call me gullible. You
won't be the first. Go ahead and call me gullible.
Frankly, look at the position I'm in. A, I'm alone, I'm
all alone, I'm, you know, I'm the last Lish, and B, okay,
there's my foot. I'm not in a good position, am I? Am
I in a good position? What I happen to be in is in a
very compromised position. It's high time we admitted this to ourselves, Gordon is in a very, very compromised position. I have to eat humble pie. We can see
this, can't we? I can see this, can't I? Gordon has to
eat humble pie. Yet I want for you to know something,
Gordon has not the slightest hesitation in him sitting

here putting you and your cohorts on notice in regards
to something—which is that they could walk in here
with their strudel, which is that they could come strid-
ing in here steaming with their trays of strudel and
strudel, but I would starve first, starve! Did you hear
me? Because I hope you heard me. But, mind you,
I have offered not one word of criticism of Aunt Lily
herself, have I? Let me, with your permission, please
beg to bring emphasis to the fact that you have not
heard from my lips me utter one shred of criticism as
far as Aunt Lily. She was a wonderful, wonderful individual. I cannot imagine a more wonderful, wonderful individual. Did I make it clear to you there was a
twinkle to her as a person? I am basing this on just
the one experience, I am admitting the fact that everything I say to you is based upon just the one and only
the one experience, but I give you every assurance, as
little as I was, as inexperienced in the rank and file of
human beings which at the time of the trip from
Woodmere to Lakewood I was, I definitely feel you
can give full faith and confidence to this statement—
which is that as a person Aunt Lily had a definite
twinkle to her which you could detect for yourself the
instant you went into the kitchen. Granted, there
might be a school of thought which would give the
credit to the light fixtures in the, you know, in the ceiling. There are people like this. Don't worry, there are

schools of thought of like every description. But if the light fixtures were responsible for it, if it was the light fixtures which were responsible for Aunt Lily's twinkle being in her, then wouldn't the other seven ladies, would not each and every one of the seven other ladies all of them standing around the table with the dough on it with Aunt Lily not also exhibit the same twinkle to them as persons? Listen, I would be the first one to acknowledge the tricks which your mind can play on you. If I thought the twinkle I saw was just a trick which my mind was playing on me then and there at that time or here and now at this one, don't think I would not admit it. I guarantee you, I would stand before you and admit it as a person free, white, and over twenty-one. No sir, you would not see me sitting here seeking to hide myself. No sir, you and your cohorts would not see me seeking to cover myself from you in my shame. The days when I was not forthcoming as an individual, believe me, since the unfortunate occurrence as far as my foot, not one leaf, not one, have I not turned over! Okay, my shoes were not forthcoming, admitted, admitted. Putting equalizers in my shoes, this was not the act of someone who could stand before you and honestly claim to be a person who was forthcoming. And then, worse, worse, going back to the shoemaker, going back to the man and telling him for him to go ahead and do it over and

make them over-compensators, fine, fine, no one can
claim this was the act of a gentleman who was dedi-
cated to him being devoted to the idea of him being
forthcoming. But I realize my error. I stand here before you bemoved by complete abjective admission of
my error. I erred! I Gordon went to lengths of extremism and in this I erred as a human being and as
a citizen and as a man and a cousin. Mea culpa. If this
is against my religion for me to say it, then I am sorry,
but mea culpa, mea culpa, if ill-bespoken. But I have
to explain something. May I please stop and please
explain something? I would really like for everybody
to stop and take the time for them to hear me explain
something. Look, is it too much for me to ask that I
be granted the simple human courtesy of somebody
explaining something? My stature is unaverage. The
fact of the matter is that my stature is below average.
So theoretically let us say what I Gordon happen to
have been doing all of these years is for me always to
walk on the sidewalk as far from the curb as it is pos-
sible for me, you know, for me to do. Let's start with
this as what we refer to as a postulate. So now the
question is what is the corollary? Because do I have
to tell you the corollary is, okay, you bump into
people? Look, let's start over again. Maybe you were
not paying close enough attention. They have the sidewalks in the city slanted, don't they? When they make

the sidewalks in the city, they slant them, don't they?
Now ask yourself, ask yourself—why is this, why is
this, why do they do this, what are they doing doing
this? All right, I'll tell you why. It's so the rain runs
off into the gutter! They do it so when the rain comes
down or so when the snow melts, it all runs off into
the gutter! Ask yourself this—if they didn't do it, if
they didn't do it, then which would happen, which?—
would there or wouldn't there be more puddles on the
sidewalk or not? So now you see. So now you know.
But what about me Gordon? How does this situation
saddle us with a ramification which concerns me Gordon? Because criers weepers, losers keepers, right?
Let me tell you something. Do I have your permission for me to tell you something? The answer could
not be simpler. The answer is staring you right in the
face. I take advantage of it! I take advantage of, you
know, of the slant! Look, it's so simple, it's so
simple—pay attention—if they make the sidewalk so
it slants down to the curb and if when you walk on
the sidewalk you walk as far away from the curb as you
can, then you are, duh, you are walking up on the high
side of the sidewalk, aren't you? So do you see my
point or do you see my point? Wait! Can you just for
a minute have the decency just to please wait for a
minute? I don't want for you to forget this—about
point, about point, about me saying the word point.

Did I or did I not tell you I once heard somebody at
Laurel in the Pines say what's the point to him or I
don't see the point to him? Or her, or maybe her.
You know when it was? It was when the Lishes were
all at Laurel in the Pines. Somebody when we were
all of us in the eating hall at Laurel in the Pines I think
said something like what is, you know, what is the
point to him or her, I don't get it, I don't get it, will
somebody please come and please explain it to me
what is the point to him or her? I don't know who
said it. I don't know who they were sitting there saying it about. All I know is it was a million million
years ago, wasn't it, wasn't it? But I keep on remembering it, don't I, don't I? Not every instant, I'm not
saying I keep on remembering it every instant. It's
only when I sit myself down to think about the trip to
Lakewood. That's when, that's when. But then the
first thing when I do is I get so upset. They had no
right to make me think it was Aunt Lily's! Maybe it
shows in me an unforgiving streak in me in my nature
for me to sit here and say this. Except I really don't
think they had any right for them to do it. Namely,
give me this impression. I had to go through a big
adjustment when I saw all Aunt Lily really was was
just a, you know, just a member of the kitchen staff.
You have to remember something. I was young. I was
little. It's like a big blow to a mere stripling of youth

for them to come to grips with a thing like this. I am not sitting here claiming it is, you know, like a big thing in the overall picture. You think I don't realize what a petty-minded position saying a thing like this places me in? It's a question of appearances, of appearances! But there is nothing petty-minded about me as a person. I am the last person in the world you would look at and say to yourself there goes a petty-minded person. Look, I am just trying to point out a facet of this which maybe you have not yet given adequate attention to yourself yet. Even I myself cannot sit here and tell if I know how close I probably was to what they refer to as a toddler in age. Didn't Abby—or Abs, Abs—say to me don't fall down over anything, Gordie? Didn't I already take the pains to get the idea of somebody being the toddler age established as far as the record, or are you sitting there forgetting Cousin Abby's admonition to me when all of the cousins were running? Because I believe I did, I believe I did. Pardon me, but nobody troubles themselves to formulate an admonition of that type like that unless the child in question happens to be somewhere more or less in the toddler range. I believe I know whereof I speak. I believe my point betokens the fact that I Gordon happen to know whereof I speak—not to mention it demonstrating I have the good grace to put my cards on the table like an adult and call a spade a spade! May

I expect you to have the same good grace as to give credit where credit is due? I was shocked beyond all fairness. I had emerged from the rumble seat, had been set down on the path, had been cautioned for me to keep to it and for me not to stray from it and step onto the grass, which I didn't, which I didn't, but for me to keep going along and going along until I Gordon came to the steps. Jesus, steps, steps! But I did this. I came to the steps. Perhaps I climbed them without assistance or, you know, or perhaps I did not. I have no particular specific recollection of it, do I, do I? But do you, do you? Am I not exercising every candor? Because I believe it may be asserted I am exercising every candor! Neither am I in a position to say what the situation was in regards to the porch. This is another blank. The porch is another blank! Step for this, steps for that? Okay, there are blanks. Granted, granted, there is the existence of, you know, of blanks. But I know there was a porch. I am firm—firm!—on this particular point of knowing in my mind there was a, you know, a porch. You will find no quibble in me as far as any number of quibbles. For instance, where was Lorraine, if you please, or Natalie, if you please? Indeed, where were any of the others on this particular point at this particular point? Or if this question is just too coarse for your inexpressibly exquisite sensibilities, then how about this one? What color car did we have? What color clothes was I wearing? What color were the various different buildings? The zinnias were yellowish. The blocks were whitewashed. There was a pattern of alteration, or of alterity, as I have stated, as I think I have taken great pains to have, you know, to have stated—rows gently curving—not winding, quote, unquote, but gently gently curving. I have been sitting here with my foot up offering these details to the record with A, with clarity, and in B, in candor. Bear in mind please, please bear in mind the excitement I was experiencing. There had been a long and an arduous—arduous!—car ride—a caravan, a caravan. We came from Woodmere! This was Lakewood! People are on vacation. Look at the whole family. I was such a child when I was a child. These are the Lishes. All I know is he gets me by the hand and he says to me wait till you see it, you will not believe it when you see it, nobody ever believes it when they see it. You know what's a miracle? Can I tell you what's a miracle? That he knew they were working on it! That's what's such a miracle. Or is it just me remembering? Am I, in my, you know, in my remembering, like skipping things? I mean, okay, what if he got me by the other hand? What if a thousand times in a row he kept getting me all set for Aunt Lily in the kitchen with the dough, but every time we, you know, we got to the kitchen there like wasn't anything happening in it? What if every time except just, you know, except for just the one time all Aunt Lily was doing was just standing around stacking trays or something? What if like a, you know, like a thousand times in a row that's how it was but if it was just the one time when he said it and we went and that that was the only time? I don't know. It's too mixed up for anybody. I think I had a point but cannot think of but mere and hurst! Or take away the dough. What if you take away the dough? Like if there was no dough for anybody for them to look up to the ceiling through, then, you know, then would I have seen the vents? You can search the most learned books, you can go to the highest mountain and search the most learned books, but I am here to tell you something—you will never find a more brilliant question than the one I just asked! I'm serious. Did you hear me? Were you listening with both ears to me? So is it any wonder I am always thinking in my mind of but mere and hurst? I'll tell you something. You want to know something? I wasn't ready for it. I definitely was not ready for it. I was too young and inexperienced for me to be ready for it. You know what? In my opinion I Gordon had not in my mind been prepared psychologically. Listen to me—I was just a cousin, I was just a person. I am the last Lish, and was, you know, was the littlest! I thought look, what is this but just a family on a family vacation? But right from the minute I emerged from the rumble seat, I was beset beset beset by impossible question after impossible question. Like step and steps! This is the thing about the whole thing of what I am sitting here telling you about. If you start with wood and wood, for instance, is there any telling where it will take you? I think people are afraid of this. I think the reason these questions have remained buried for so many eras is that human beings are like afraid of them and get nervous in their minds from them. It's really regrettable. Frankly, it is a very sad thing to me personally. They let the untold rewards which could be theirs, and which could, you know, that could have profound implications for all of humanity at large, become overpowered by their terror of tampering with the unknown and the unforseen and the untoward. Look at me, look at me, sitting here scared to death about the medal which I couldn't even ask anybody about it in regards to it at the time to its religious orientation. And you know what? Suppose it didn't have any? I mean, how do we know it had any? There was no basis for such a, you know, for such a postulate, now was there? All the years and the years of it, eras and eras—the waste of it, so much disgusting and useless time wasted, my God, it's so personally discouraging to me. I'm old now. I have let my life go up in what they refer to as smoke. I have let myself sit here and get frantic over things which are, you know, which are a thing of the past. Whereas meanwhile, whereas what about the feelings I have as far as walking past people on the sidewalk when all of the time I might have just gone ahead spending my time thinking about getting somewhere? The girlfriend I mentioned to you—did I mention to you this girlfriend I used to have to you? What did it get me? Did it get me anything the way they say you can go to the bank with? Did it get me anything like lasting or durable? Granted, there was a nice facet to her or two, but let's get serious and look at the overall picture as far as these so-called facets. Excuse me. I have to interrupt this to tell you something. There happens to have been somewhere between let's say a three-hour and a four-hour interruption in this. From writing facets to writing this, there has been this, you know, this very exasperating terrible experience which I have just had and which I am well aware I should keep to myself, which I am well aware of I would be better advised for me to keep it to myself, but which I'm sorry, I'm sorry, but which it has really had this terrible effect upon how I feel about sitting here writing this. I have to tell you, everybody, I have to tell you I happen to find myself in a very exasperated mood right now, and I think it is definitely going to have a very deleterious effect on things. Frankly, I'm trembling.

I'm sorry to involve you in this, but I want to be honest with you, there is every reason for me to be fair and aboveboard with you, and it is in this spirit of aboveboardness, it is in this very spirit of me and my fidelity to aboveboardness that I sit here and tell you I am absolutely absolutely absolutely trembling. All right, here is the story. The story is I felt I needed a snack. I had this feeling I should probably go get myself a snack of something. So I go to the kitchen and I go get out my bowl and I get out my corn flakes and I get my spoon and I go to get the carton of milk and I start bobbling it. So are you acquainted with this word? You are familiar or conversant with this word? I am bobbling it and it's meanwhile flying out of the spout all over everywhere, like almost a whole entire carton of milk from bobbling it. So this is what the interruption which I was telling you about is all about. I'm supposed to be in here with my foot up writing and instead I'm like, you know, I'm in there in the kitchen with rags in the kitchen. It went everywhere. You didn't even know there were places anything could get to like this until it got to them. I'm serious. There are like these new places which have heretofore never before existed before because of milk not ever befouling them before. But the part of it which has left me really feeling so touchy-feeling about it is this hobble and bobble thing, or bobble and hobble. So

did you ever? I tell you, I'm trembling. You could
feel it if you touched me—trembling, positively trembling! Is it the weirdest or is it the weirdest? No kidding. Because if let's say I sat down and dared to go
ahead and speak of this to some individual who, you
know, who did not know me as well as you do and
was not as conversant and familiar with me as you are,
what do you honestly think their, you know, their re-
action would be? Do I have to tell you? I don't have
to tell you, do I? Regular people, they just look at it
and they say to themselves so okay, so hobble and
bobble, so what? I mean, regular people, to them it
stands to reason, you hurt your foot, you hobble—you
got a carton of milk which gets away from you, so
okay, so you bobble. The thing to regular people is
you go ahead and take these things like this in stride.
Whereas individuals like us who write books and so
on, forget it, whatever it is, we're so vicarious about it,
always standing there and taking everything so to heart.
But you know what? It's high time we cut it out. Am
I right or am I right? This extremes thing, this always
going so overboard thing, it's high time we sat ourselves
down and came to our senses and, you know, and cut
it out. Because it wears you out. It takes everything
out of you, going to lengths. You know what it is?
Can I tell you what it is? It's draining. It is definitely
very draining. And meanwhile since when does it ben-

efit anyone? Not one person in the whole human race derives the least little benefit from it. You know what you end up with? Let me tell you what you end up with. You end up with nervous exhaustion. Is this what I want for myself as a human being, ending up with nervous exhaustion? All right, harlequinade, gasconade, so what? So one minute she's Iris, the next she's Wanda, so what? So Lorraine and Natalie, so what? You know what Cousin Buddy's real name was? It was Norman! Okay, it was Norman, so what? Look, I am going to tell you what my problem is. I go ahead and give myself much too much latitude. I don't keep myself on a tight enough rein. I don't keep myself on, you know, on course. I see the pocket watch. I'm on the way to the pocket watch. I've got the grapple bucket positioned right over the pocket watch. And then, poof, my mind goes ahead and sees something else it wants. And you know what this kind of problem is the result of? I Gordon am too smart for my own good! This is the problem in a nutshell. Except I'm telling you, it's a relief for me to finally actually see it. I am sitting here breathing like a sigh of relief for me finally to have the clarity of mind and clear-mindedness for me finally to see what has been going on with me since the day I was born. It's like, okay, it's like a great stone has been lifted up like off of my chest. Or would I have been better off if I had said back? Would this whole passage in here have all of it gone ahead and read better for you as a reader if I had held my tongue and given it a little more, you know, more thought and not said chest but said back? I'll tell you something. This should really be a lesson to us. I'm sorry, but we should all of us strive to learn from these experiences and to extract the personal lesson which is in them for us as individuals— your foot, your corn flakes, your milk, all this hobble one minute, then some bobble the next, not to mention the medal on the one hand and the pirate on the other. Or wait a minute, wait a minute—didn't we decide in our minds buccaneer or privateer? Boy, if only she could see me now. That, you know, that so-called ex-girlfriend of mine. Or do I mean Natalie? I don't know. Does it make any difference? Nothing makes any difference when the next thing you know is you turn around and all it is is it's hobble and bobble, bobble and hobble. But shame on me, shame on me. We were the same religion, weren't we? You know what this means? I mean, for two people for them to be the same religion as each other. I grew up in Woodmere. She grew up in Cedarhurst. So we are, we're not only like A, the same religion, but B, B, we both, you know, we both come from towns which are like right next to each other almost—Woodmere and Cedarhurst, Cedarhurst and Woodmere. Which even more incredible, which even more incredible, it's like, you know, it's like Jesus, it's like Lakewood and Lakehurst, right? Wait a minute, wait a minute, I'm looking up hurst. I'm stopping this and I'm getting up and I'm looking up hurst. No, forget it. It won't have hurst. Besides, my foot. Did I tell you Buddy's real name was Norman? How about the fact that Cousin Jerry, that Cousin Jerry, that his real name was Jonathan? So what was I saying? Wasn't I saying something about her and Abby's place? Remember Cousin Abby? Cousin Abby's the cousin who said Gordie, Gordie, watch where you're running! He was my favorite, Cousin Abby. Abs. You know, Abs. Another name we had for him in the family for him, it was Abs. So anyway, so the thing is Abs let's us use his place. It's like, you know, it's like ages later, it's like a lifetime later, and guess what. Abs let's us use his place. Oh sure sure sure sure, I told you about the keys already, I told you about the keys already, did I or did I not? There were five of them! Were there not five of them? Look, use your intelligence for once. Try to exercise your intelligence just for once. Don't sit there like a lump on a bump constantly leaning on me for every little thing on me. This is a two-way street, is it not? One hand washes the other, does it not? Don't I have my hands full as it is? There is only so much I Gordon as a novelist can do. I am only hu-

man, you know. Try to show some, you know, some
consideration for someone other than yourself for once.
She could, she could—she could get her legs turned
out for you! She had this way which she could do
where she could get her legs turned out for you in
such a way as for her to get her nishy opened up all
of the way open for you. I mean, you knew you were
in, you know? I'm serious. You really knew you were
in! There wasn't any question but that, you know, but
that you were in. I mean, you know—she let you, she
let you! Not like the way it is with, you know, with
like some of them, you know. Not like with those
ones which act like oh hey are you in there yet, don't
forget to let me know if you are in there yet, make
sure you give me the high sign when you want for me
to actually be aware of the fact now you're actually in
there yet. Oh come on, you know how some of them
are. Do I have to sit here and tell you how some of
them are? Look alive, for Christ's sake, and don't
make me sit here and look like an idiot. Listen, you
know what my theory is? Can I tell you what my
theory is? They turn their feet the other way so their,
you know, so like their legs, you know, so like they go
ahead and follow in suit. You see what I'm saying? It's
subtle. It's really subtle. It's maybe too subtle a thing
for your average reader to sit there like a lump on a
bump and detect, but I'm serious, I'm serious—it's like

they can like lie there on their backs and like rotate them or something. So does this make sense? Because I think it's like, you know, they can either rotate them so it either opens up the nishy for you for you to get it in all of the way in or it doesn't. It's like there's this adjustment they can make, depending. It's like they can get it very very subtly adjusted, depending on how they feel about it or something. I'm telling you, it's not your nozzle, it's not. But that's what they want you to think, isn't it? I mean, it's the whole idea of it, isn't it?—trying to get you to think it's all in the nozzle, but I'm telling you it's not, it's not! My God, there are so many things like this. You want to know something? It's impossible to count them all, it's impossible for you to keep up with them all—the minute you spot one, the minute you spot one they go ahead and figure out two more of them for them to put there for them to take its place. We're fighting a losing battle. I don't know if you have noticed this or not, but honestly honestly, we are honestly fighting a losing battle. You do your best. You try your best. You go ahead and focus your entire attention—but what's the use? There's too many of them. You turn around and you know what? There's another one! Barrette is one. Did I mention that barrette, that barrette's one? And in cellophane, wrapped in this wrapping of cellophane, a hair ribbon, a hair ribbon!

Oh, beribboned—I really am really a very big fan of, you know, of beribboned. No kidding, all of these be-something words, all of them, all of them—like, you know, like bestride and so forth—I love them, I love them. Hey, I'm just nuts about words. Which is why I'm a novelist—it's, you know, it's why I am a novelist, from being so crazy in love with words. Would you believe it, the fact that I am still sitting here upset about cry? What page was that? They're all on the floor. They've all of them been skidding off of the table and going, you know, and going and falling onto the floor. This table's not big enough. This is the first thing which worried me about this, that this table would not be big enough. I've got to get a better dictionary. The minute my foot's better, you know what? I'm getting myself a better dictionary. I deserve a better dictionary. A human being crazy about words as much as I am, I think they deserve to have a better dictionary. Okay okay okay okay—I get myself up out of the rumble seat, or somebody comes and gets me up out of the rumble seat and sets me down right between the first set of blocks and then next, there's next there's this first set of flowers. Forget it. I can't do it. It's just an act. This is no good. Aren't I just faking it? How can these be the things? All these are are only just the words. Camellias, camellias—so lonely-looking, so whitewashed. Little Eugene was actually big-

ger than Big Eugene. They just called Big Eugene Big
Eugene because Big Eugene was born first. Plus the
fact they also called him Euge sometimes, Big Eugene.
You know what I think? I think there was something
in it, not calling her Big Reggie. I'm serious. It
would not have been respectful acting. Or do you
think it was a slur, the Lishes not calling my mother
Big Reggie when the other Reggie came second? You
think it's what you get when you're a Deutsch and not
a Lish? It's like Aunt Lily not being a Deutsch and not
a Lish and not being the owner of anything. She had
to carry trays. She had to fix the dough. She was not
even in charge of it when they made it. She was just
one of the ladies all standing around the table. He
took me by the hand. He got me by the hand. He
said to me Gordie, the next thing you see is going to
be something which you will never forget as a person
you saw. It was bigger than the table. It kept getting
bigger than the table. It kept getting bigger and getting bigger until it was getting to come off down over
the, you know, down over the sides of the table. They
kept lifting it up and catching the air in it up under
the underneath of it and then letting it come down
back down again on top of the table again until it kept
coming back down on the top of it with more and
more of it hanging down over the sides of it. It was
unbelievable. It was so unbelievable. It was like

catching everything in the world up inside of itself and
then, you know, and then like coming back down and
then being calm again and then being settled and calm.
The Deutsches, oh the Deutsches, did you know I
never came across not even one other of them except
A, my mother, and, you know, and B, me Gordon?
Here's what she did. Here is what she did. She went
to the door and said what do you want? She said for
everybody for them to get under the bed and then
went to the door and said what do you want? I could
hear her. Everybody could hear her. We could hear
her. When she said consider yourself kissed, they all
must have heard her. Everybody was kissing hello.
The whole family was all kissing hello. But maybe it
was, you know, maybe it was just a joke. Doesn't it
sound to you like it could have been just a joke? You
probably don't even believe it about my foot. Or believe how come was it it was their names which stayed
the same—Aunt Dora and so on. Because that's inter-
esting, isn't it? I mean, why do they do that, change
the names of some people and not change the names
of other people? Try it yourself sometime, sitting writing with your foot. Even with a cushion under it, even
when somebody has a cushion under it, you think it's
not a torment? Just the position alone is more than
your average individual could stand to handle. I give
the credit to my family. They're the ones who get the

credit. People wouldn't believe it if they knew what I am dealing with. I misjudged you. I judged you vicariously. I failed to attribute to you full faith and so forth. This is a common mistake. I do not exonerate myself. I do not exculpate myself. I simply say as a human being this will not happen again —nor will it hereinafter. Isn't there the word colonnade? Or how about cockade? I think there is one of those words cockade or colonnade. And escapade, there is escapade—and barricade and blockade and blockade and barricade—and didn't I probably miss grenade, didn't I? Don't ask me what flavor strudel it was. I do not know what flavor strudel it was. It did not matter to me how they all of them raved over it. It actually made me sick how they all of them always sat there always raving over it. Not that I was the sole cousin not to, you know, not to partake of it. All of the Lish cousins partook of it not. Listen to me—the word was terrible. The steam was terrible. It was terrible seeing Aunt Lily with a tray of it. Wait a minute, wait a minute—did you know it got thin enough for you to look up and see through it to, you know, to what was up on the other side of it in the ceiling? Here is my thinking. You want to hear my thinking? I am going to tell you my thinking. The filth in them, the filth—up in the vents, up in the vents—was there anything to keep it from, you know, from like from it coming down

and getting down on things the same way it, you know,
it went up? What was there for there to keep this
from happening? There was not anything anywhere in
the kitchen to keep this from happening. Let me ask
you something. Can I ask you something? Does it or
does it not stand to reason? This is all I want to know.
I want to know yes or no yes or no yes or no. I want
you to think this thing through in your mind for me
and then answer me the question it does or does not
in your, you know, in your mind stand or not stand to
reason to you. Stop. Stop reading for a minute. I'm
serious, stop reading, stop reading! Peter. I said I'm
the last Lish, I sat here and said in no uncertain terms
to you I am the last Lish—but it was only for me not
to have to get into the whole thing of, you know, of
Peter. Because, okay, Peter—Peter Lish, he is the last
Lish—and this time I'm serious, I'm really serious.
Because it wasn't Abby's place, it wasn't Abby's place—
it was really Peter's. It's been on my conscience. It's
been on my conscience and been bothering my conscience. Maybe it's why my mind could not think of
what else to go where cry went. Neither does this
mean I have not bestriven myself to everywhere else
tell the truth. Believe me, I Gordon do not shirk from
facts. You will never find me Gordon shirking from
the facts. Who looked through the dough? Did I look
through the dough? I didn't have to, did I? But I did,

didn't I! Okay, I am sorry for prevaricating. The place was Peter's. It was not Cousin Abs's for his girlfriends. The place was Abs's son's Peter's. Listen, it's names, not persons. All of them, they're just, you know, just names, not persons. There is probably some kind of an air current in here. It feels to me like there's probably this very subtle turbulence of air being turbulent in the air in here. I hate this, the air. I hate human beings. Believe me, I could name some. But why give them the publicity? Peter, for instance, the way he asked for his keys back—shame on him, shame! You know what it was? Can I tell you what it was? It was a pigsty, that's what it was! It makes me ashamed to have to tell you, a Lish. Even a Deutsch. Ventilation vents or not, even a Deutsch. I honestly can't believe I am sitting here telling you a Lish made his residence into such a pigsty. Thank goodness his father did not have to live for him to have to hear me say this. It would have probably killed the man for him to have to live to hear somebody say this. The man was, I want to tell you this, the man was good to me. It's terrible that I Gordon should have to be the vehicle for people for this to get out to them. You know what he used to say to me, Abs? When we were all of us all running. All of the cousins, all of the cousins, we're running, we're running! So guess what he used to say to me, Abs, Abby, my favorite cousin. "Watch it you do not fall, Gordie! Be careful you do not fall over anything, Gordie!" How many cousins would say a thing to you like this? You think it would be so easy for you to find yourself a cousin anywhere all over the place who would say a thing like this to you, even a girl cousin? The Lishes, the Lishes, what a family! What I wouldn't give for us to all of us to be getting packed up all over again all in our cars again all as a family again on our way from Woodmere or even from Cedarhurst again to Lakewood or even to Lakehurst again. You know what Lakehurst was? Did I tell you what Lakehurst was? Lakehurst was the town next door to Lakewood. You know how Cedarhurst was to Woodmere—next door? That's how Lakehurst was to Lakewood, next door. They were both the town next door. But who as a family was next door to us in the cabin next door to us? Well, it was probably Lishes, it was probably just more Lishes. Like Uncle Henry's or Uncle Charlie's or Uncle Sam's—like, you know, like their Lishes. The men with horses with guns with holsters with rags all around them tied all around them, all they wanted was water. You know what they wanted? Because all they wanted was water. You could hear her say all you want is water? You could hear her say to them you only want some water? It was incredible for me. I am not kidding with you. A thing like this, I did not know a thing like this could

just come out from nowhere and be at your door.
Nobody ever told me a thing like this could just do
this. They should have stood there and besought to
explain it all to me beforehand—instead of making me
sit in the car making me think in the rumble seat she
owned it. How come nobody said to me for me to
get set for soldiers on bivouac on maneuver or maneuvers? But no no no no no no—come see what's in the
kitchen Gordie come see what is going on in the
kitchen Gordie you will not believe it what is happening in the kitchen Gordie! Or Gordon—Abs said
Gordie, they said Gordon. Plus she said Gordie. Plus
her. But no no no no no no—they come take you by
your hand and they say to you for you to get set not
for the horses at the door with holsters with holsters
but for the dough spreading out from all over itself in
the kitchen on the table. It's unforgivable. I'm sorry,
but I'm telling you it's, you know, it is personally unforgivable. This is why I could not forgive them. Because it is namely, because it is unforgivable. You
know what they went to their graves without? They
went to their graves without any forgiveness from me.
This is what the two of them went to their graves without. I promise you, they had it coming. If anybody
had it coming, then they were the ones who did! How
dare they! You know what I say? I say how dare they!
Granted, granted, he came and got under the bed with

us just the same way we did. But does this exonerate him? Since when does this exculpate him? In a
pig's eye it does! I'm going to tell you something.
You want for me to tell you something? Nobody is
getting away with what they did to me when they
didn't have to! And I'll tell you something else. Are
you ready for something else? Abs, Abby, this so-called,
you know, this so-called cousin of mine, what exactly
was it did he think he was talking about—fall, fall?
What was there to fall over? What was there for anybody to fall over? You know, it was like there was just
grass, just grass! All of the way to the arcade from the
eating hall, what was there but just the porch you went
across, then the steps you went down, then the walkway you went along, then the rest of the way to the
arcade, wasn't it just grass? How come was it there
was this idea which he had in his mind that I Gordon
would be the one to fall down? Where did this come
from, fall, fall? The bastard had a lot of crust to say
fall. How does this get to the root of the problem?
Does it help anybody for them to go ahead and root
out the problem for them to say elevate to you? Believe me, nobody came to me and offered me the
benefit of their better judgment as far as which side of
the sidewalk it made sense for me as a pedestrian to
walk on. Not from one individual did I receive the
least shred of, you know, of guidance from. I had to

look for myself, I had to see for myself, I had to figure out the whole entire ramification of the situation
all by myself. But do I get credit for it? Is there one
individual who comes to me and stands there and gives
me any credit for it? I could drop dead holding my
breath waiting for any of them to give me the least
little shred of credit for it. What I get instead of credit
is them walking into me! What I get instead of credit
is people complaining I Gordon am going against the
traffic! It's batty to call people walking traffic. I never
heard of it, calling people walking traffic. Because,
mind you, I am not unprepared to be elucidated. I
have never shown myself unprepared to be elucidated.
Let them come forward, then. Let them look me in
the face and address me like a civilized person and say
to me there's been some changes made, get used to
them. I am only too happy and glad to learn. No one
wants a new lease on life more than I do. I could go
on for who knows how long so long as this foot does
not turn invidious on me. He must be crazy, ice.
That's crazy, ice. I tried ice. It's too cold, ice. It makes
no sense, ice. They should take his license away.
There should be a committee which should get together and take his license away. The crust of the man,
the crust—sends you a statement for elevate and ice.
Am I made of money? I am not made of money!
You think first. You weigh first. You consider. You

take into consideration. What I worry about is this—
suppose they said let's look in your shoes? Would
there be anything to stop him from saying to me let's
take a look in your shoes? It could get blabbed all
around. They can't wait for them to have something
for them to blab it all around. It's what they're all of
them there for in the first place, going around blab-
bing it all around. You want me to tell you what's a
mystery to me? It's a mystery to me whether you
bought this book or went ahead and got it at the library. Because I could name you where you give them
your money and you, you know, you hear the time running out the instant you give it to them. I mean it—
it's whirring or it is ticking. Whirring's different.
Whirring's more like something is beating instead of
ticking, which is more like stopping and starting—isn't
it, ticking? Maybe a thing like this, it's probably over
the head of the reader. Wait a minute. I'm Jewish.
Did I tell you I'm Jewish? We were Jewish. The Lishes
were Jewish. But okay, but since when does this have
to mean that, you know, that I Gordon have to have
ill-natured feelings for whatever religion you are? It
doesn't, does it? Or do you hold it against me as far
as the fact all of the families at Laurel in the Pines were
probably Jewish people going on a Jewish holiday?
Because I take it back, the word vacation. So that's vacation and cry, I take them both back. Plus saying it

was Abby or Abs when the truth was it was Peter. Besides, I was scared, is probably why. Listen, it all made
me scared—writing this, going places. Mere and hurst,
hurst and mere. Even before I put the penny in, even
before I put my penny in, even when we all of us first
just got there and I Gordon was the youngest—never
mind, I can't finish this sentence, I have lost all of my
interest in, you know, in finishing this sentence. They
had wrappings on them. Did I tell you they had wrappings on them? I'm serious, I'm serious. The horses
or the holsters, it was like, you know, it was like rags,
I think. I'm almost positive, I think. Give me a
minute—a barrette, a barrette, a comb, a necklace, a
pin to go on your dress, this kind of jewel thing to go
on your dress. Wanda, Little Reggie, Iris, Lorraine,
Natalie. A hair ribbon for your hair. Cellophane, to
see something in cellophane—you can't believe it, you
wouldn't believe it, what it meant to you for you to so
many eras upon eras ago to see something in cellophane! What a thrill it was, something in cellophane.
What a thrill it was what a thrill it was—just the word
thrill! But they stand there and look you in the face
like you are some kind of, you know, like you are
some kind of a psycho or something. This is the state
we're in with the English language. I have to hang my
head in lament in regards to the state we're in with the
English language. I'm glad there are no more Lishes.

You know what? It makes me glad I'm the last of the Lishes. Or that Peter is. I'm telling you, they can all of them go thank their lucky stars they did not live to see the state the English language is in. Whatever it cost you to get this book, or if you didn't shell out any fucking shekels for it but instead you got it on loan or something from some kind of a fucking library or something, believe me, you're better off. You know that junky metal which is like, you know, like nearmetal? Or like this metal-like substance? Things just don't have that iron feeling which they used to have, do they? Or a steel one? Be honest with yourself! Wait a minute, one more minute, give me another minute—marinade! And I said pomade, didn't I? Didn't I say charade and pomade? Oh my God, what I just thought of! I cannot believe what I just thought of! My God, it's a miracle I Gordon—Gordon!— Gordo!—am still sitting here still in one piece. Because I'm sorry I'm sorry, but it was the most exciting thing to me, there was nothing which was ever even a little bit more of an exciting thing to me the arcade was the most exciting thing in my life to me. Unless it was the Treasure Chest itself. Or, you know, or the Buried Treasure. Or her when I went with her to Peter's. Truthfully can I tell you something truthfully? Because I do not begrudge him asking me for the keys back despite the fact which I would not require the services of a lawyer or of an attorney for me to prove to the satisfaction of the authorities Jewish or otherwise he of his own personal accord without coercion nor unlawful inducement made over to me as a private citizen free white and twenty-one legally gained copies of quality of notwithstanding. But I give you my word my word—iron these were not! Not one out of all five of them was worth the paper it was written on! I pour out my heart to you. I Gordon sit here pouring out my heart to you like it's the last minute of my life to you, and this this this this is what I get for it? I get stares for it? I get stared at like an ignoramus sits there staring at you for it? Do I deserve this? Are these the deserts I am supposed to sit here and deserve for this? Did I or did I not sit myself down here with the best of intentions? My heart is wide open, isn't it? I know I left out steel! My heart was reaching out, wasn't it? I wanted to share, didn't I? Do I or do I not have your permission to remind you where my foot is? But the cards were stacked against me, weren't they? There never was a prayer of success, was there? Just first of all just what about the fact of me first of all being Jewish! Oh sure oh sure didn't think I would stoop so low as to, you know, as to sit here and make mention of it, did you, did you? Plus also forget about the fact of me sitting here with my foot, for instance. Forget finally okay, forget please the fact of the table being too ridiculously small of a table for me to do anything worth doing at it to begin with. Consider, I ask for you to please consider the ugly nature of people. You treat them like they have feelings. But this is your big mistake. You know what interests them? I will tell you what interests them. Feathering their nests! Feathering their own nests! Going out and looking for feathers for their own personal nests! This is what interests people and why the human race is in the state it's in. I tried my best. I approached you with such candor it makes me sick. Name me one other human being who would sit themselves down and open up their heart as far as bespangle or bestraddle. I'm dealing with brutes. Admit it—brutes! I Gordon have written books upon books, but it's like the individuals which get their hands on them, forget it, they are brutes. I'm sorry I'm sorry but excuse me excuse me—did you pay the regular price for this book? Or did you get it for something off? This wouldn't happen to be some copy of it you got for something off, would it? Did you get this out of some filthy dirty bin somewhere? You didn't steal it, did you? I Gordon am sitting here sweating bullets thinking what to put where cry and vacation went and you are sitting there with a stolen book? My God, is this the way the world works or is this the way the world works? I'm just some kind of a, you know, of a jerk to you, aren't I? I am sitting here beset by a foot up just so you can sit in comfort smirking to yourself as regards me and my religion and bestrewn! My God my God my God it was bestrewn down there, bestrewn! In the sand in the sand, it was all bestrewn. A pencil. A thimble. There were or there weren't needles? Maybe all it was was a little tiny mending kit. Maybe it was just a tiny little mending kit. His sword was thrust up. The privateer in the corner down there, they had a privateer down there in a corner down in there—a sword that curved cruelly and was thrust up! A cutlass was it? Did they not call it a cutlass? Does the dictionary not call it a cutlass? And brigand, he was a brigand! Scoundrel! Her nishy, you want to hear what her word for her nishy was? Zeezee! It was zeezee! She called it her zeezee! It was a new one on me, I can tell you. I never ran into any of them before who ever theretofore called it before a zeezee before. I'm telling you, it was incredible incredible incredible incredible—her getting her nishy arranged for you in like this like this opened out at you way she had of hers meanwhile whispering it to me in my ear to me get it in me up in my zeezee Gordie, get it all of the way in me up. Where did she get it from? Where do people get things like this from? Do you have any idea where somebody could go ahead and get a thing like this from? It made me

feel so funny-feeling, zeezee. Plus I do not even want
to discuss it with you as far as her going in there into
this so-called facility of his. Words fail me. May I say
something? Words fail me. Believe me, there are limits. I do not jest with you. This is, you know, it's not
any jape with you. Let me ask you something. Am I
wrong? At least meet me halfway. Am I asking for the
moon? I have shown good faith. You did or did not
see me turn the other cheek? Or does this just make
me more invidious in your eyes? Listen, maybe you
should know something. Maybe this is the ideal time
for you to know something. Which is that she came
with a washcloth! What does this betoken? What does
this bespeak? You know what there was? Can I tell
you what there was? Because there was this idea in my
mind they would all love me for me having a big vocabulary. But was I so wrong to think that? Don't
worry, I could name you some names. Never think I
Gordon cannot throw caution to the wind and name
you some names! Fine, fine, I am going to tell you
something. Because it just so happens I did not tell
you the whole truth as far as me walking around the
block. All right, I fell down. Because this is a perfect
example of what you have to go through. Plus what's
my next step? Do I keep going and just go to what I
was going to say next or do I sit here thinking and
cogitating? It's a struggle. It's a constant struggle. On

top of which it's thankless. People don't care. You show them something like mere and hurst and they look you in the face like you are stark raving mad. Hobble and bobble, bobble and hobble, my God, it's insanity, readers reading like it was business as, you know, as usual. The average person probably looks at the word zeezee and thinks to themselves okay so what's so wrong with that? Believe me, if I made the rules, it would be a different story from start to finish. Listen, if I made the rules, you think there wouldn't be a law against the fact of them being allowed to have only one laurel in there in all of those pines? There would be a law against a lot of the things your public is getting away with and which nobody but a handful of well-situated individuals would stand there and have the courage to tell you about. I could name names, don't kid yourself. But things are buried. They're not buried all of the way, no. They're not, you know, completely buried under things, no. My God, how could they be completely? Stop and think for a minute, how for Christ's sake. How about you stop and use your brains for a minute, for bleeding Christ's sake? Things can't be buried completely down under anything. Because Jesus Jesus if that's what they were, could you see them enough for anybody to know what they wanted? You wouldn't even be able for you to know what it was you wanted if they were! Bestrewn,

bestrewn, they have got them all bestrewn but you can
see them a little bit. They're only, you know, like bur-
ied-ish. I don't think this elevation is doing a thing for
it. I don't think this elevation advice they gave me is
adding up to meaning a thing for it. Frankly, it's kill-
ing me. Go ahead and sit like I'm sitting and see for
yourself if you like could fucking write something! So
how do you think she picked up the trick of doing it
like that? Because it was like she could turn her legs
so like it let you be able for you to get your nozzle up
inside of her nishy max. She was one in a million. As
far as this facet, I'm telling you, she was honestly one
in a million. Some of them, they act like okay they
want you all of the way up there, but take it from me,
it's just a, you know, it's just an act. Whereas the gang
of them, they will look you right in the face and stand
there and tell you to the contrary. Or like lie there, or
lie there. The point is, what the point is is this—they
do something. I'm serious I'm serious—they have this
way of them doing something. I don't know. It's
probably from these very little, you know, from these
tiny tiny little adjustments which they are always doing. It lets you get up in them in their nishy, all right.
But it keeps you out to where, you know, like to
where like the slash itself is! I can't put it into words.
But you know what I mean. They all of them do it.
It takes one in a million of them for her not to lie

there or lay there and fucking do it. What's behind the
whole thing I Gordon have racked my brains upon
and do not know. Not that I do not have my theories,
of course. I mean, one minute you say to yourself okay
it's because your nozzle just so happens to be so extensive like they can't lie there or lay there and take
this much of it up in them and so they're like, you
know, they're like automatically call it protecting themselves like shying away like. Then the next minute I
think who knows who knows who knows, don't throw
stones at anybody because who knows if it's not actually this intimacy issue the whole public is always making such an issue over. But another thing there's bound
to be this one particular specific percentage of them
which are trying to foist off on you this idea they have
of whatever you happen to have in this department as
far as a nozzle, forget it, it's, you know, it's inconsequen-
tial. You know this kind. They really burn me up,
this kind. They say things to you like would you
please let me know when you're in. They go ahead
and say things to you like okay like are you in yet?
Or let me know when you're in. Or tell me if you're
in. Or give me the high sign when you think you're
in. But not her, not her. It was really quite a facet
about her. Did you know we used to have a time
limit? We used to have a time limit. We always had
a time limit. It was like okay she has to get back to

where she lives and I have to get back to somewhere
else too, or Peter coming back or Peter coming back.
But what does not have a limit of time to it? I'm telling you, this is the nature of things, a limit of time to
it! I'm sorry I'm sorry but did you borrow this book
and not give it back? Truthfully are you using this
book vicariously like from some library or something?
Because I Gordon am fed up to the gills with this
ceaseless fucking vicaritude. You will not believe what
I just went ahead and made up my mind for me to
leave out of this book for me instead to sit here and,
you know, and teach you people a lesson about this
constant ceaseless vicaritude. Sure it's bestrewn sure it's
bestrewn how could it not be bestrewn? But since
when does this mean every Tom Dick and Harry can
just come along walking along and, you know, and just
whistle you a merry tune? Pay attention! There were
lilies when you went walking along along the sides of
it or rows. Or Aunt—stem, stem, like a stem, a
flower—it was

Rose with the dough in the kitchen, or Aunt Rose with the dough in the kitchen! Oh yes yes yes I thought not! There was a machine like a game. Things inside of it were inside of glass. It had a brigand in it with a cutlass in it. Thrust up in your way— oh my God oh my God, the cruelly curving blade! Quick, quick, pick which title is your pick as far as a title. Or how about *Towards a Better Blank*? Looking

back on it, it was my job for me to get the pic of
Abby—of Abs, of Abs!—back up over the bed on the
wall. You think you could have done it with a pic of
him up there? Don't kid yourself don't kid yourself
you and your whole family couldn't have done it with
a pic of anybody up over the bed on the wall anywhere! Listen, I'm going to ask you a question. Can
I ask you a question? Which was it you did, which,
which—all at once, one at a time, or in clumps? Dirty
filthy fucking readers with nothing for them to sit and
do but hurt your fucking feelings! Instead of cry, instead of cry, what about instead of cry lie down and kill
people? Don't ask me to, you know, to explain it. Listen, it doesn't make any sense I know it doesn't make
any sense but if you think about it in your mind for
enough it starts to it starts to and then once it starts to
then everything else does everything does does. Petu-
nias or something or foxglove foxglove—like these
lonely-looking melancholy-looking foxglove—first a
foxglove, then like this big block of something with
like this nice fresh-looking clean-looking like whitewash all over it. It tore my heart out. I'm telling you,
it tore my heart out! I had such a feeling from it, there
was such a feeling in me from it that it started seep-
ing around in me through inside of me from it. It was
such a feeling. I did not want to move anymore. I did
not want to keep going all along the walkway any-

more. I just wanted to lie down and for me to kill
people. You see what I mean? So you see what I
mean? It was everything—the steps next, it was having to go get to the steps next, it was having for me
to go ahead and get to the steps next and not step on
anything I wasn't supposed to between—plus the rows
of them, it was all of this being in between them as far
as, you know, as them being like these rows of them
with them winding like that. Or what did I say, didn't
I say didn't I say did I not say curving like that? Ever
so cruelly! Look, are these begonias I'm talking about
or gardenias? These tall tall scared-looking things, like
they were going to faint and fall down and, you know,
and kill people—like they were wounded or something
or had a fever or something and wanted to kill people
for something. It's too complicated. You probably
don't have the brains for it. I do not have anything
against you personally. It's just that people just don't
have the brains for it. They do the best they can. I'm
not saying they do not do the best they can. But a
thing like this is way past the power of people as far
as comprehension or understanding. The next thing
you know they turn around and call you mental. You
want me to explain something to you? Okay, I am
going to go ahead and explain something to you. It
was cruelly curving. It curled cruelly. Its curl, the
walkway's or the path's, it was cruel. Okay? I mean,

duh, it has to do with, you know, with these things like this. But look at me, this genius with this foot like this. I should have picked a bigger table. What was I thinking when I picked this particular specific table? I did not utilize enough foresight. I should have employed more foresight. If I had the brains I was born with, I would have A, I would have utilized more intelligence, and B, employed more foresight. You need to see the sides of it and meanwhile see ahead. This is what you need—to see the sides and see ahead. On the other hand, if you know the strudel is coming, isn't the whole meal wrecked? Oh yes oh yes oh yes, I make no secret of the fact—none, none!—of the fact that, you know, that I was the youngest and that I was the littlest. But don't forget the fact oh no oh no you had better not stand there and forget the fact that I Gordon am what you would call extensively built down there—extensively! It didn't do her any good for her to change her name. Everybody has a right to their theory, and I'm sorry, I'm sorry but this includes me too, you know. Now, now, come, come, there, there—metaphorically speaking, of course. Well, they were never the same after they came to the door. You know what? Can I tell you what? Nobody was the same after they came to the door! Remember them coming to the door? Granted, granted, all it was was the United States Army of America but they came to the door, they came to the door! It finished him in regards to her telling him for him to get under the bed. It finished all of us for us to hear her tell him get under the bed. The die was cast. This was the thing with it—the fact that the die was cast with it. But what choice did she have? Didn't she know he wanted for her to say it? You know what I think? You want for me to tell you what I Gordon think? Because I Gordon think she only said it so he could say to himself I am, you know, I am only doing this because she said it. It probably was like a peace-of-mind issue. You see what I'm saying? There is no question in my mind as far as this being what they probably call a peace-of-mind issue. The minute they were there at the door with their various different things, there wasn't any way out for anybody, was there? There were like these holsters but maybe not with guns, maybe with just with rags like it was maybe bandages on them and not guns in them. I don't know. I sit here and say to myself it was eras and eras ago. But I was always very patriotic. I am very patriotic. I Gordon am a regular demon when it comes to, you know, to me being patriotic. It's one of the things about me—like having like this pretty incredible vocabulary on the one hand and yet being pretty extensive down there even though me being short of stature on the other hand. I would walk more if I was more taller.

I'm serious. It's just these things these things in my shoes, they're really murder on you if you go ahead and try it for any distance. Some people, they walk around the town. Some people, they take the whole day and they go walk around the town. But what about around the block? Hey, please, is it about patriotism or is it about patriotism? But now look—criers weepers, losers keepers! Okay, question time. So yes or no yes or no yes or no, are you and your staff ready for another, you know, like another question time? So zeezee or zizi, which? I'm serious, which is it, which is it, is it zeezee or is it zizi, which? Because my God my God, I Gordon can't just call her up and ask her, can I? Couldn't he answer? He could answer. Wow, what if it was, you know, if I called up to find out if you spell her nishy this way or that way and it went ahead and was him which answered? Fine, fine, I am just, you know, just taking a guess and keeping on saying zeezee for this. But is there any telling like okay like how in her mind she thought she was personally spelling it? Or do you think it gives people a lot more of the feeling of an actual nishy if they spell it zizi instead of zeezee? Oh Jesus oh Jesus wait a minute wait a minute! What are we going to do if he picks this up and reads this? Or suppose she says to herself okay I am going to fix this little prick with this big extensive widdler of his and then she goes out and gets this and goes ahead and gives it to him for him to read it and then for him to come get me when he sees it spelt whichever way I go ahead and decide in my mind for me to spell it! What then, what then? With my name on it and everything! Jesus! Or like she just shows him just this page, for instance and like not any of the pages with all of the things on them about, you know, about other things like Laurel in the Pines, for instance, but just points with her fingernail to where I spelt it the way I spelt it and goes ahead and says to him look look you see you see who else calls her thing a thing like this like zeezee like zizi who else who else? Oh, assassins assassins killers they're all killers they are all lilies they're all are

roses. Point, point, let them all fucking point! Because, duh, it just so happens I Gordon happen to see the point to me! Because okay so what if he comes and kills me? Wouldn't I get to be so famous for it? Hey, face facts, I'd get to be famous as a novelist for it! Who wrote zeezee who wrote zizi I did I did! Who could tell you they were going to get killed for writing zeezee or zizi I did I did! I'm sorry I'm sorry but so how's this for being a, you know, for somebody being a novelist! Not to mention not even putting anything on the pages when I Gordon just don't happen to feel like putting anything on the pages! But be this as it may an individual who desires for them to be a novelist still needs

grammar and vocabulary. Let's face it, you can't get together a novel for people without grammar and vocabulary, can you?—plus A candor and B clarity. Look,
there was a lot of emotional feeling for us aside from
just the factor of just us just lying there and having
sexual intercourse on a one-to-one basis as individuals with each other. You know what I could not get
over? I could not get over the way she rolled out the
welcome mat for you. Because she really rolled it out
for you. I also could not get over was she lying or laying. I'm going to tell you something. I really loved
it having sexual intercourse together with her the way
she always went ahead with her legs and, you know,
and really rolled out the welcome mat for you. You
could really get somewhere with an individual like
her. She was not the kind of human being to lay there
and try to pull on you any of those fucking stunts I
told you about. You want A clarity and B candor? Because I will be only too happy and glad to, you know,
for me to sit here and give you A clarity and B candor. For example for example you take the fact I went
ahead against every shred of intelligent advice and
skipped pages didn't I didn't I? But ask yourself why.
Did you stop and give me the benefit of the doubt and,
you know, and honestly ask yourself why? Or do you
think pages like that that all they do is like defeat their
own purpose? Fine fine but see the point see the

point? Because okay because he sees me say zeezee
or zizi and he comes and gets me. So this means the
novel which after this I Gordon was getting all set to
write, the whole thing of it was going to be all of
these blank pages which were going to be in it but if
I'm dead if I'm dead then in all candor and clarity then
like what's the deal with them then as far as me first
with blank pages? Because, you know, because doesn't
it really wreck these plans I had with myself like about
writing a novel like it before there was anybody else
which went ahead and wrote a novel like it, like pages
and pages with nothing written on them except maybe
if I felt like it just the page numbers or not even the
page numbers on them? But on the other hand on
the other hand if he kills me from zeezee if he kills
me from zizi then aren't I amn't I still the most famous? Or is it your personal opinion an idea like this
is, you know, that it's like way off of the deep end? I
don't know. I sit here and I have to tell you I honestly as the author of this just cannot get myself to go
ahead and decide in my mind. Like cry and so forth.
Or vacation. Like do I go for the barrette if I can't, you
know, if there is like no way for me to stand there and
get anything else, plus the medal? But meanwhile
meanwhile the whole deal is it's whirring on you. Or,
you know, or it is ticking on you—the pages turning
somebody coming along and like turning the pages on

you one at a time on you or all at once on you or in
Jesus in Jesus in clumps. Listen, you know what I date
the whole breakdown in this to? Because I date the
whole breakdown in this to when I went ahead from
the equalizers to the over-compensators! Or attribute,
attribute. Right there, right there! It was then and
there that I have to say to you I attribute it to it as far
as everything going around the bend. Come come
now now there there, I Gordon going waltzing back in
there into the shoemaker's to say to the man okay let's
go ahead and go to some serious lengths as far as this
extremism. So when will I learn? Is enough never
enough for me? They told me. They warned me.
Not a day goes by that I do not still hear them plead-
ing with me in my mind's ear, "Gordie, darling, please,
darling, pay attention, darling—moderation is a virtue."
But what can you do with people? It's hopeless. You
simply have to sit there and take them as they come.
Live and let live, this is the only intelligent policy for
an intelligent person. And I'll tell you something
else—people are people, whatever their walk of life!
There is not a one of them which does not want to
stand there and take the path of least resistance! Look
at me, for instance. I am the author of this book, for
instance—but does this mean I should be allowed to
be immune from following the rules everybody else
has to follow? I promise you, I Gordon am far from

perfect. People think I am above the fray over all of
the various different ills just because of the fact that I
am the author. But I promise you, I Gordon am far
from perfect. May I give you some advice? Don't put
me on a pedestal! In all reality, I am just as, you know,
as pathetic as you are. If I told you some of the things
I could tell you, what is the first thing you would say
to yourself? You would say to yourself yes yes he is the
author of this but he is just as pathetic as we ourselves
are. You know what? This is the United States of
America. You know what else? If anybody needed a
pedestal, if there was anybody who could have stood
there and been, you know, been better off with a pedestal, then we don't have to sit here and guess who, do
we? Because I'm serious, I had all I could do just for
me to reach up and reach the handle, let alone for me
to be tall enough to see down into the bottom of it
and, you know, be able to tell where all the bestrewing
left everything laying. Or lying. Did I tell you he had
a patch over his eye? Did I tell you he had an
eyepatch? And grapple bucket, grapple bucket, I only
said grapple bucket because the dictionary said for me
to. Listen, you want to know something? Claw, what
it looked like was like a claw! So in a manner of
speaking, all I am saying is even if a person is the author, they still have to let the dictionary have its due.
But be this as it may, everybody is entitled to go ahead

and have these emotional feelings which come over us.
It's only human. It's just the nature which we have as
human beings. Please—things do not roll off our back
like a duck. You know what I say? I say let these
emotional feelings out! I say bottling them up, it's going to lead to health issues. I Gordon am not a doc-
tor, but this does not mean I do not happen to know
what's good for people. For instance, it made my, you
know, my skin crawl when she went in there into his
facility for her to get her zeezee wiped off. I'm serious. It made me jump out of my skin, the filth in
there as far as a facility. And another thing, the pic of
Abby, the pic of Abs, a person, what kind of a person
could keep their mind thinking straight as far as a situation of this type? The time element and so forth.
Like a constant ceaseless time limit! Everything would
always be too much of a time thing for me. Steps have
to be taken, plus measures must be enacted. And that's
downplaying it! That is definitely downplaying it! You
know the word befall? Because I would just like to
reassure myself you are conversant and familiar with the
word befall. Believe me, it is such a funny-acting thing.
You have to be so careful as the author. You cannot be
too careful as the author. One word, the, you know,
the most unbelievably innocent word, and skip it. You
have to remember you as the author can never say to
yourself okay I as the author am above the fray as far

as the dictionary. Plus timing. Timing is a whole different issue even all by itself even. But I'll tell you something about timing. I am going to tell you something about timing. Timing's like inborn. You have to be, you know, be born with it. It's like an inborn thing. It has to be born into you. It is either born into you or forget it. I had to learn this. It was a bitter lesson. If it taught me anything, if my experience with the Buried Treasure or with the Treasure Chest taught me anything, it is the fact that somebody can't go by the ticking or by the whirring as the way it's going to go exclusively. They count. Ticking or whirring. It's not the fact that ticking or whirring don't count. Because nobody is claiming your mind can just go ahead and discount a thing like ticking or whirring when you are standing there going crazy dealing with the fucking handle. Wait a minute wait a minute stop everything for a minute please stop everything for a minute! Because I Gordon can't betoken it anymore I can't I can't the fact I sat here and said grapple bucket when claw it felt like claw it was a claw because it felt like claw! Plus the time was going to be up plus can't I hear it going in there down inside in there whirr whirr or tick tick plus look what happened as far as cry and vacation. My penny! Can I say something? My penny! And that's the truth! So try to learn from my experience. Try to profit from it. Don't be a jerk. There is no excuse for you to just be a jerk. But woe betide the human being that has this idea in their mind they can rely upon inspiration ninety-nine percent of the time! In other words, I don't care how much of a genius you personally are, you cannot just sit around and say to everybody okay look at me with my foot up. You have to earn the breaks. You have to put your back into it. You have to, you know, to go around the block. In other words criers weepers losers keepers am I right or am I right? Wait wait! I just thought of something I just thought of something. It's about promenade and, you know, and crusade! Because don't you remember don't you remember we're thinking about all of these ade words and be words? Unless this is too deep for you. So is it too deep for you? Because it's nothing to be ashamed of if it's, you know, if it's like, you know, too deep for you. On the other hand, nobody put a gun to your head to make you get this book, did they? Listen, there's plenty of fish in the sea, don't forget. Look at me, do I know what mere means? Or like what hurst in something means? But you don't hear me fucking bitching about it like a fucking crybaby, do you? The whole thing is knowing what the score is. It's like listening to something nobody else is. Which is what it is when you're supposed to be the author of it. Because there's always this time limit. The whole thing of it is you have to listen, you have to keep listening for this thing like this time limit. Does she have to get home at some point yes or no yes or no? You can't just lay there or lie there and go to lengths forever, you know. There are limits, you know. You name it, there's like always this like limit, you know. Get the locks unlocked, get your things off, get the pic of Abby or of Abs down off of the, you know, of the wall. You know what I'm sorry about? I Gordon am sitting here sorry about the fact I never told her anything about Lakewood. It was so wonderful. Lakewood and Lakehurst and Laurel in the Pines. I felt so thrilled with myself! Until there were these lilies along the walkway. My God, so cruel! Then you had to keep going and not step anywhere until you got to the steps of something. Then Jesus Jesus Aunt Rose they take you by your hand they come and take you by this hand or it was maybe they take you by this other hand and they say to you wait until you see Aunt Rose making strudel for everybody in the kitchen! Hey, answer me this—when he comes and gets me for this, then won't I be like the author who sat down and wrote out their own, you know, like their own personal death warrant? Well, of course, of course, I could take it out! Couldn't I get down on the floor and go through all of the pages and take out all of the zeezees and zizis out? Cushion's not as good as pillow anyway. So how come I did not have the brains in my head not to make it cushion but make it pillow? I made a mistake not making it pillow. And not saying betake yet. And getting it wrong as far as cry and vacation, right? You know what it is? It's all just this Lishes and Deutsches, Deutsches and Lishes! Five keys for you to get yourself into a fucking pigsty tell me when you ever heard of something as fucking crazy as five keys for it. But could she roll out the welcome mat for you! You know what? She could really go ahead and roll out the old, you know, the old welcome mat for you! But I have to tell you something I have to tell you something—you could see through it. I could see through it. When it was up there, anybody could come into the kitchen and see up into the air and see through it. My God it didn't fit it anymore, how was it going to come down and be able to fit it anymore, it wasn't going to be able for it to ever fit it anymore, but did this stop them? Does this ever stop them? No no no no no no no it does not stop them, it does not stop them. They just keep sailing it right back up there back up into the air again, him screaming at me, him shrieking at me, everybody shrieking at me, everybody shrieking at me, "Gordie, Gordie, sonny boy, sonny boy, do you see it, do you see it?" Look, let me ask you something. I want to ask you something. What would have been so hard for them for them to say instead Gordo? Except you know what it looked like? Can I tell you what it looked like? Because it looked like he was standing like standing guard over it! They're against the Jews. You can tell it when you see them all thrust up like that— the fact that what they're against is the Jews. Always whirring underneath them like that. Always ticking. Whether it be on bivouac on maneuver or whether it be maneuvers. Kill me did I think about kill me I did not think about kill me I had not thought about kill me I wasn't sitting here thinking about kill me when I sat down here and started getting everything together for this novel. *Towards a Better Blank.* Isn't this what, duh, this is? Except shouldn't somebody probably better get rid of the page numbers and of the stuff up at the top of the pages? I could see up I could see up, but I was too small for me to see down to the bottom of it where they were all of them all bestrewn all over the bottom of it. Truth be told, to get the penny in, I had to reach up so to speak up on my toes for me to get the penny in. There was a slot. You put your penny in the slot. Then the whole thing of it was then was just the handle! Which it felt to me like it had this iron feeling to it. Or steel. Everything did. Even the marigolds did. It all felt to me like it was hard on account of something and by itself on account of something and could knock me down because of it. There wasn't anything which did not look to me like steps

must be taken, like measures enacted. We all of us
started screaming. All they wanted was water, wasn't
it? She said water? Didn't she say water? You could
hear her say to them all you say you want is water?
You could hear her say to them you say you only just
want just some water? But all of the families in the
eating hall, they all were all of them acting like it was
funny, like it was hysterical, like it was, you know, like
it was so hilarious or just like some big kind of a joke
or something which happened as far as the United
States Army of America when it was a Jewish holiday
for the Lishes in Lakewood and the only Deutsch the
whole Passover was my mother! Plus Aunt Rose with
all this flour all over her! Listen, you want to know
why I'm a nervous wreck? Forget it. Criers weepers,
losers keepers! Meanwhile, you think for one instant
I Gordon am not pretty lucky I never once fell out of
their rumble seat? Fine, fine—he said ice, try ice, and
elevation, give it elevation. Social hall! Jesus Jesus,
should have been calling it social hall calling it social
hall not calling it eating hall but social. Come come
now now there there! Honest mistake. Another thing
is leaving out key-ring and leaving out barrette. Or
maybe it was key-chain I left out and not barrette!
Plus there was this little tiny toy mirror for if you were,
you know, like one of the girl cousins. Plus there was
a magnifying glass. Plus there were these other

things—like a comb probably. These things for your
hair probably. Probably a timepiece, a bracelet, probably a medal. You put your penny in. You get up
when the strudel is coming and you go around the
table and there are your aunts and there are your
uncles and there is your mother and there is your father and there is Sister Natalie there is your Sister
Natalie and Lorraine and Iris and Kenny and Wanda
and Big Eugene and Little Eugene and Jonathan and
Jerry and Ruthie and Reggie and Reggie and Iris and
Kenneth and Kenny and Big Gene and Little Gene
and Buddy and Norman and Norman and Buddy and
Charlie and Phillie and Dora and Sam and Dora and
Miriam and Henry and Abs and Abby and Gordie and
Euge and Esther and Esther's Abbot whom they called
Abs whom Abs whom Peter or Peter plus Aunt God
love her may she rest in peace Aunt—no, Tante,
Tante!—Rose. Jesus Christ twinkle she twinkled, my
dead Tante Rose, befloured befloured. Am stopping to
put foot down okay have got foot down. Because hurst
is one thing, but mere, you know, mere is another. So
is sullage. So as the reader, so are you, do you think,
are you all off on account of eating hall instead of social? How about grapple bucket? Or Buried Treasure
when it probably would have been better if it said
Treasure Chest? But am I Gordon sitting here holding anything against the shoemaker? It's just a, duh,

it's, you know, it's only just a novel. It's not a real
sidewalk. I mean, like the sidewalk, it's not like it's
any real sidewalk, is it? Even if it's slanted sideways.
It's toothed. It has these teeth. There are like these
teeth and, you know, like cables. It's like it has jaws
you could probably call them. The whole thing comes
down and comes down and then plunges. A claw! I'll
tell you what I wanted. You know what I wanted?
Okay, so here is a list of what they had. They had a
jackknife. They had like a barrette and probably a
jackknife! I'm sorry, but what a welcome mat! God,
Jesus God, wouldn't it be wonderful if she was right
here right this instant for her to lay down or lie down
and like really get to show me how an individual
could really go ahead and like get the old welcome
mat all, you know, all rolled out for you. You think I
Gordon jest? I Gordon do not jest. This is no jape.
I make no jape. We were a great family. We were the
greatest family. We had two Eugenes, for Christ's sake!
Listen, I have a theory. You want to hear my theory?
It was our downfall. That's my theory. You just heard
my theory. So what do you think? Was that too many
names or was that too many names? Lish and Deutsch,
Deutsch and Lish—it's just too many names even for
anything. Because nothing could stop her with her
zeezee for her nishy and her washcloth! Well, what do
we have so far? Did we have steaming? Did we have

strudel? Please, in regards to people having feelings for
a fellow human being, you people are the jape as far
as any jape around here! Heaven forbid I Gordon
should have to sit here and not get my foot cut off for
you or something. No no no no no no no it is not
enough somebody stands there to be slain for you oh
no no no no no no let them first come and cut off my,
you know, how about just to begin with a foot for you!
Listen, you know what I would like to do? I would
like to wash my hands of the whole affair. Truthfully,
may I speak truthfully? I never should have got myself involved. You know what? Can I tell you what?
It's the wrong table. It never was the right table. I'm
telling you I'm telling you in my mind in my mind I
knew it right from the start of this in my mind I was
handling it all wrong right from the start of this in my
mind. Well, I was misled. I could not possibly not
possibly have been more as an author misled. Did I
tell you they made me think it was her place? I'm telling you they kept making me think it was her place.
It wasn't fair for them to make me think anything
which wasn't fair. My God, it looked to me like she
had to work all of the time with flour on her all of the
time just for her even to be somewhere. Plus another
thing—you reached all of the way up and put a penny
in. I remember the thing they had. I remember how
everything was this different kind of a, you know, of a

thing they had! Here's a list of them. Here is a list! Hurst, for instance—mere, for instance. I Gordon can give you a list! You want a list? Here's a

list. Genius!—
page after page of genius and what credit do I get for
it? Yet come ye to me door, me precious—ah, come
ye to me door! This privateer of ours—brigand, brig-
and, buccaneer! God, how they come and come and
betake it from you. Are you even born yet? You are
not even alive for them to come and spot you by your
vocabulary yet let alone by even your grammar yet and
yet still the scoundrels come and rob you blind for it,
dictionaries aforethought! I don't know. I just don't
have the digestion for it anymore. Limit to everything,
you know. Not even this goes on forever, you know.
How much you pay for this? You pay anything for this?
You paid for how many more pages of this? Want to
hear a list? Here's a list. Avast ye, yar! Unlock it,
then lock it back up, unlock it, then lock it back up,
unlock it, then lock it back up, unlock it, then lock it
back up, unlock it, then lock it back up. Plus time the
time for just for getting the pic of him down and then
for getting the pic of him back up. Did I say butter-
cup? So lovely. So lovely-looking. Forget it—heart
wasn't in it anyway. No real pep in me left in me for
it anyway. No feeling left in me anyway. Want the
truth? Tell you the truth. It was all of it Deutsches.
We were all of us Deutsches. The idea was for us to

go get us to see the famous wreckage of something in Lindenhurst at an airfield in Lindenhurst. It was a Jewish holiday or something. Maybe it was Passover. We got on some buses. We had to keep changing buses. It took us forever and it got to be too late and we turned around and we got back on the same buses and we all went back to Cedarhurst and we had chicken salad sandwiches and hamburgers in Bea's Tea Room. They kept saying we would try it again. But we never tried it again. I don't care. I don't miss anything. Not seeing the wreckage of something doesn't make me feel like I really should feel upset-feeling about anything missing anything. What got me going was going to Lindenhurst from, you know, from Cedarhurst. I mean, the names of things. All I like really is just like the names of things. Like, you know— like Lakewood, like Woodmere. And pines and laurels and laurels and pines. And one only laurel in all of the pines. Christians, I wish we had all of us been Christians. Belaureled. The way it is, I don't even you know I do not even like walking on the sidewalk. Hey, did I tell you what I do? I keep to the inside of it. I keep to the high side of it. Because it's fixed, they've got it fixed so that the water, so that it runs down from off up high down to the curb and then off into, and then down off into the, you know, the gutter. This is what happens. You see what happens? You sit down

and A, you've got mere, and then B, B, next it's hurst.
No wonder your mind can't think straight. Is it any
wonder your mind it's all beguiled? I mean, honestly
honestly, whoever saw a curving so cruel? Please, the
least shred of intelligence, if my mind had been thinking with the least shred of intelligence, I would have
sat here and said to myself Gordo goldenrods—goldenrods Gordo goldenrods. So yes or no or yes or no,
Gordo does or doesn't sound to you more like, you
know, like more befitting-sounding? But what good
does it do when they lay there and they say to you
when they lie there and they say to you are you in yet
are you in yet tell me when you really think you have
really got it all of the way in me yet? Not that she ever
did! Man oh man the thing of it with her was she
was all of her all welcome mat. So did I or didn't I
tell you I had a sister Louella who went ahead and
changed her name to Loretta but who everybody kept
calling her Lou or whom? She killed herself. She
killed herself. She took pills and killed herself. Reason it is getting mentioned is in case you or your family are of the opinion I Gordon probably have some
explaining to do as far as me looking like I was trying instead of for the jackknife for the barrette. God,
the feeling of it the feeling of it going along between
the gladiolas and these blocks with like somebody put
this white whitewash all over them. The thing I love

next to this is this thing of me being the author of this. Granted, granted, the table is not right and my foot is all wrong, but I just love it when you can sit yourself down and say the table is not right and say my foot is all wrong and say who is this knocking at my door? Just kidding. Just jesting around with these various different vicarious japes of mine which keep coming up on me on account of the fact pages do. I'm sorry I'm sorry, but these are the lengths these are the extremisms this is what the scoundrels keep asking of an individual when they have gone ahead and like devised their genus cried sufficiency conspired to befuddle those who would in the rumble seat deem to have deemed the steps to be taken the measures enacted. You know what? It better be one. A virtue. Moderation. For how not fall when one has gotten themselves up, mad inner soles into the bargain?

A LATER TRY OR A TRY LATER

YOU KNOW THIS THING they used to have? They used to have this thing that had these things down inside of it. You remember how you used to go to this place and there would be all of these various different vicarious things there and there would be this one thing which they would have there and it would have all of these various different vicarious things down inside of it down there down in the bottom of it? It was glass. The top of it was glass. It was like a tank of glass on top of this iron thing or call it iron-looking thing and the whole idea of it in going there was putting a penny in and then going ahead and working this claw thing which they had in it up in the top of it and getting it to come down and come down and try to get up one of these things which were down inside of it all laid out all over it on the sand or in the sand or even almost all of the way under it as far as certain cases of certain things. This was the whole idea of it, getting one of these things with like like these jaws sort of which were toothed sort of. So do you or don't you remember it—this thing I'm talking about with the sand and the penny and the things? Because I remember it and remember it that they called it the Akades, which was this hotel they had

somewhere for the Jews.
Did anybody ever go look up gasconade? Would
somebody please make themselves a note for them to
do it? Because I don't want to have to ask twice. It's

not nice for you to make anybody for them to have to
ask for anything twice. I am the youngest. I am the
smallest. This is why I walk where I walk and have to
suffer on account of my shoes. I forgot the girls. They
probably all killed themselves as far as I am concerned.
I was the one who got kissed. There was no point to
the rest of anyone. You'd look and you'd say to yourself so okay so what is the point to any of them would
somebody please come tell me what is supposed to be
in anybody's opinion the point to them? Hey, can I
tell you something? Let me tell you something.
Which is that, you know, that no matter how far you
get it in, no matter how far they ever let you get it in,
you are never, so to speak, are you ever, so to speak,
ever getting all of the way in with it ever? Or even far
enough? Was it something unwinding? It sounded to
me like there was this unwinding sound of something
unwinding. But I did not have the hands for it. I did
not have the feet for it. I did not have the digestion
for it the brains for it the desire for it. Here is what
I wanted. You know what I wanted? I wanted for me
not to have to make believe I wanted something. But
there were like these cables or things. It looked to me
like there were like these make-believe cables and
things. Plus in the corner with like these high-buckle
shoes like a doll, I think. It would really slam down.
It would really plunge. Do you know what I mean

when I say plunge? There were chains. You'd hear the chains—and then it would open up and open up and then there would be more teeth and then the teeth would go ahead and bite this big terrible bite out of anything. Come come now now there there, you remember! Don't try to hand me this crap you don't remember! Everybody remembers. They had like this little toy doll in it in a corner in it. The word swashbuckler is coming to me, the word swashbuckler! He was above the fray of everything. He was so thrilling. There was never anything so thrilling. Tante Natalie in the kitchen and the ladies in the kitchen getting the air in up under the dough, Tante Natalie in the kitchen and the ladies in the kitchen getting the dough lifted up to get the air in up under it! I don't want to finish the sentence. There is no percentage in it for me as far as me finishing the sentence. Or trying for me to go get to the vents and sit here and describe for you the vents—the grates, the flues!—way up above up there up above everything everybody was doing. I'm telling you, I'm telling you—gashes!—they were dirty filthy gashes up there up back behind the dough. Or didn't I tell you the thinner it got the thinner it got the more you could the more you could, like you know, like Jesus Jesus like see what was back up there back up behind the dough? Can I take you into my confidence? I never got down and made like particular

specific measurements of like high to low and so on!
I never actually like just got down with like instru-
ments and so on and in so many words just like made
measurements of it or something! But doesn't it take
for you to do that this kind of sine or cosine or something? Don't you have to have with you some kind of
a thing like a sine or a cosine or something? Hey,
come on, slanted or canted, I go only as far as, you
know, only as far as the words go. I mean, if that's it
for the words, then that's it for Captain Gordo, isn't it?
One question, can I ask you please just one more question please? The dirty filthy crap up there, you think
me seeing it, you think there is any chance of the fact
of them getting me to stand there and see it, you think
this was maybe like the whole thing with all of them
from the beginning? I mean like you look through
the dictionary and you see pasquinade is what I
mean—one at a time or all at once or all in all these
vicious nasty clumps is what I mean.

LAST TRY EVER TRY

I HURT MY FOOT from not from any falling thing.

Not from any shoe thing either.

It was just from somebody steps on it.

Somebody says to me can't you see how come you can't see you're on the wrong side of everything and, you know, and then they step on it.

Somebody says to me hey, big guy, don't act like you don't know which side is the wrong side.

And goes ahead and does it on it.

So much for going for a block.

Yeah, and something else I'll tell you—the whole thing of it's who's got the buckles on whose shoes?

A WORD FROM,

YOU KNOW,

FROM THE AUTHOR OF THIS

I'M SORRY, BUT ISN'T IT HIGH TIME there was a statement fighting back against them always accusing me of never writing novels but only of, you know, of me sitting here keeping trying to get away with these like these sort of like thinly—thinly, I said—don't they always say thinly?—these sort of like thinly disguised autobiographies, if you will or wouldn't? Because it is a dirty stinking rotten lie! Like you take everything in this book, it is all of it made-up—whereas in life the only actual like real-life thing I ever had anything to do with as far as an arcade was as far as with a completely different kind of a one. It was the walk-through kind of a one. It was the kind of a one where you go from one street to another street by walking through this kind of a tunnel which is sort of like built up over you this curvy ceiling up above you. Oh, what a thing it was—like with shops and with newsstands and with places for you to eat at all along the way on either side of you as you go. Or, you know, or went. Because it is this kind of an arcade which is the only kind of an arcade which I ever really had any actual contact with as far as any actual event in my life. Whereas this other kind of an arcade, the kind of an arcade where they had all of these various different vicarious games for you and things—like let's say an amusement arcade or like an arcade where amusement is the idea of it as far as the arcade—all of these individuals all going all around amusing themselves—I never had any of what you might reasonably go ahead and classify for yourself as any direct actual true experience with anything like an arcade like that kind of an arcade, much as I as the author of this am definitely prepared to say I would like to have liked to. But the walk-through kind, oh the walk-through kind—there was here in the city right here in the city one of these walk-through kinds and where it was was at Fourteen Hundred Broadway and I what I did there was have lots of true-to-life real-life times in my life at it at one which was just like that kind of an arcade. Because the kind of arcade at Fourteen Hundred Broadway was the kind of arcade where I used to get taken to to go out to go have lunch with my father when I would go visit my father at my father's office, which was in this big powerful building which was at 65 West 39th Street on all of these many, many floors. Because my father was powerful, my father was so powerful, my father was very powerful! My father was, Jesus, I thought my father was the boss of everything, and this was the greatest thing there ever was for me, this was such a terrific thing for me—because it made me feel like I was the son of the boss of everything and the Captain Gordo of all my games. Oh my father, he made neckerchiefs and bandanas and bandanas and neckerchiefs for ladies! My father was the biggest maker there was of

neckerchiefs and bandanas and of bandanas and neckerchiefs for ladies! I'm serious. If you went somewhere and you saw somebody there with a neckerchief or with a bandana there, ducks will get you
drakes it was my father which probably was the maker
of it. The name of the company was Regal Manufac-
turing because it was named after my mother, whose
name was Regina, and the place where my father and
I were always going to get ourselves like a bite of
something for us to eat when it was okay for my father for him to go out and maybe for him get away for
a little bit from everybody always calling for him oh
Phil Lish oh Phil Lish oh could you come take a look
at this bandana or neckerchief Phil Lish, it, this place,
its name, the name of it, was Jimmy's. Hey, did I love
Jimmy's! Honest, I was just so crazy for, you know, for
Jimmy's. To this day I swear it to you—to this day as
the author of this I swear this to you—never have I ever
loved anything I ever loved as much as when down we
would go the two of us down in the elevator in my
father's big building and go down to Jimmy's! Did I
tell you it was in this arcade at Fourteen Hundred
Broadway—Jimmy's, that Jimmy's was?—and that for
us to get down in the elevator and then for us to get
back up in the elevator that there was this dwarf from
he said it was Malta who took us? That's where it was,
that's where this place we ate at was—it was like in

took us? That's where it was, that's where this place
we ate at was—it was like in this, you know, in this
sort of like tunnel which went from between the
middle of one street to between the middle of another
street and which I'm positive they called it an arcade.
Anyway, from Malta—didn't I say from Malta? And
hot corned beef and hot brisket and hot pastrami—this
was the deal as far as the sandwiches which you could
get and all you could get at Jimmy's if you went to
Jimmy's was just, you know, sandwiches. Whereas everybody else whereas all of the other people who
were everybody else, they all had to have to have meat
loaf and have to have lettuce and have to have chicken
dishes and, you know, and eat in the light of day and
have to eat in the light of day and have to go ahead
and get their bite of what it was they were going there
eating at places like Schrafft's or at Child's or Ham-
burger Heaven.

Oh, Jimmy's or Teddy's or if Euge's it was!

But the two of us, we went down into it and came
back up from down under in it rich, say rich!—I and
my boss of a father stepping along all at once in the
United States of America—beladen, say beladen!—
steaming plunderers of the offered earth, treasure ahead
of us, ravishment behind—thrusting up from down in
the bottom of my first and last arcade.

HOW TO WRITE A NOVEL

YOU NEED LISHES.

You need a family of Lishes.

Or, okay, or of Deutsches.

You need them always saying to you what in the name of God is it which is the matter with you, always twisting, always constantly twisting, forever incessantly twisting, never not for an instant not twisting every single word?

You need Lishes who never miss a minute to say to you sweetheart, what is it with you, what could conceivably be the point to you, nothing never not turned upside down with you never not inside out with you never not mixed up from frontwards to backwards to forwards with you, not to mention still all over again still sideways plus sidewards with you.

Is it spite?

Is this what it is with you, it's spite?

Why can't you talk like a normal human being?

Why is it when we ask you a particular specific intelligent question we get an answer no individual could begin to make one iota of sense out of right from like the word go?

You heard of the word concoct?

Darling, they made it up for just for you, concoct.

Cockeyed in plain language, did it never exist until present company came and did everybody a favor to us of gracing us with his presence?

Dear reader, dear reader—dear writer, dear writer—let me ask you can I ask you who could argue could I argue with I could not argue could I?

Meanwhile, you know what?

Because here's what.

Work on your blanks and go get the medal.

Plus never sit still for strudel.

Nor look up not hurst nor mere but see the high grates up in the high grilles up in the high grates get the rodomontade of gummy bemirings spread back along back up to the high flange that has to have itself hinged up high up high enough in the vent enough, else how else does the flanging of everything ever get itself flanged?

Fine, fine—now consider yourself kissed.

Then with luck luck scribble and be killed.

What is the imperative
in things
and the imperative
that we have to perceive things?

—ALPHONSO LINGIS

THIS PAGE,
HITHERTO BLANK,
OWES ITS REDEMPTION,
TO THE UNBLANKITUDE OF
NINA ROSENWALD.

Some actual Lishes
the author of this ordinarily knows about:

JENNY

BECKY

ETHAN

ILENE

NINA

ISAAC

ANNE

And here's three Mutnicks:

ANDREW

PEARL

EZRA

How about a Marx and a Spiotta?

PATRICIA AND DANA, OR PATTY

And not also an Andreou and a Lentricchia?

GEORGE AND FRANK, OR FRANK AND GEORGE

Hey, hey, where's the Ozick?

AS IN CYNTHIA!